PREFECTING THE PRIESTHOOD

A SPECULATIVE FICTION NOVELLA

THE NEXT HIGH PRIEST SERIES

BOOK 7

PETER DEHAAN

- Copyeditor: Robyn Mulder
- Cover design: Fanderclai Design
- Author photo: Chelsie Jensen Photography

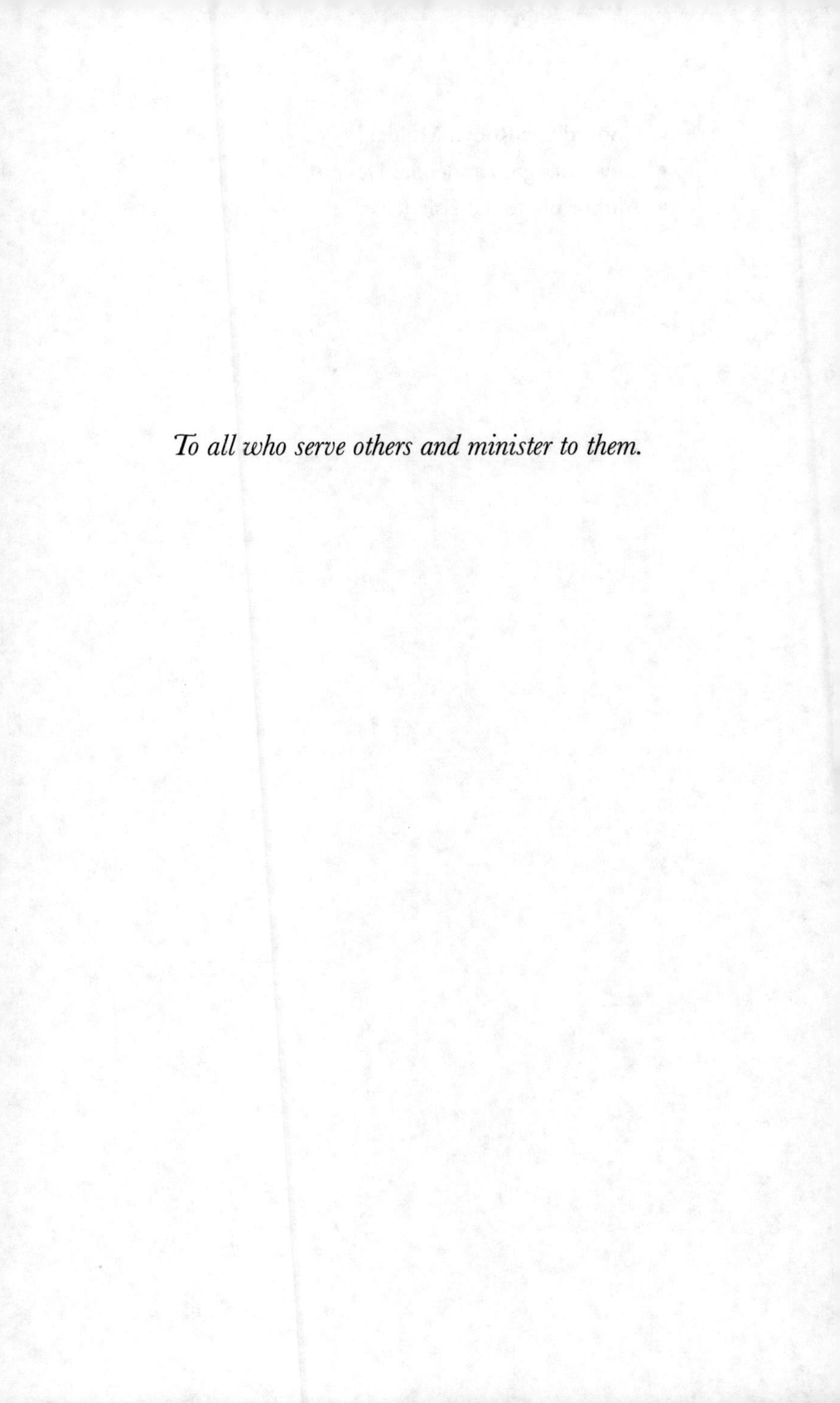

To all who serve others and minister to them.

CONTENTS

PERFECTING THE PRIESTHOOD

In a world just like ours . . . only different.

I desire faithful shepherds who love me and care for my flock. They will be my priests, and I will be their Lord. - Prophecy 38.104

1: A FRESH START

Emma watched the officers lead the handcuffed Barney Clark away. This time he'd be gone for good. She knew that for sure. The Sovereign had told her.

Between her feet stood a trembling Montgomery. The tiny puppy's tail was tucked tightly between his rear legs. He whimpered at the sight of his master being hauled away.

"I think we're finally rid of him," said Fred, Emma's executive admin. Then he glanced at her and cocked his head to the side. "You're not about to cry, are you?"

Emma shook her head. "No. I just wonder how things might have turned out had he made better decisions. When he wasn't scheming behind my back, he was a good aide. Quite good."

"We can certainly find you another aide."

"I don't need one. I've got you and the rest of the team to help me in my role here at the Temple as High Priestess. We made up the aide position just so we could keep tabs on him. I'm more worried about Montgomery. He doesn't understand what just happened, but he knows it was something bad. He's terrified. Just look at him shaking."

As Fred glanced at Montgomery, cowering between Emma's feet, she bent down and scooped up the tiny pup. "It's okay, little buddy. I'll take care of you. Don't worry."

"From the beginning, he's taken a shine to you," Fred said. "So you've got that going for you, but what do you know about taking care of dogs?"

"Not much," Emma admitted. "But I know just who can help." She ruffled the fur on Montgomery's head, and he received her affection with delight, his tail wagging for the first time since his master had been carted off. "Let's go visit Auntie Ashley."

Fred shook his head. "Auntie Ashley?"

Emma giggled. "Maybe I'm more of a dog person than I realized." Emma lowered

Montgomery to the ground and turned to go visit the cosmetologist. Montgomery trotted along beside her, his head bobbing with each step.

Emma reached the salon and opened the door. Angie—who had helped Emma free the prisoners—sat in the chair with Ashley standing next to her. Startled, they stopped talking and froze. Ashley turned red, while Angie's face blanched. They both stared at Emma, unblinking.

"Sorry to interrupt," Emma said. "I'll try later." She stepped back, but Ashley stopped her. "No worries. We're done. Just having some girl talk."

Emma studied each woman. Angie was almost old enough to be Ashley's grandmother. What would a seasoned nurse have in common with a 19-year-old cosmetologist? Emma waited for Ashley to say more, something the young woman excelled at, but she remained silent. Emma had definitely interrupted something important.

Angie stood. "I was just leaving," she said to Emma. Then she turned to Ashley. "We'll talk more later." She gave Ashley a sly wink. Then the amiable nurse left the salon.

That's when Ashley noticed Montgomery. "Oh! How exciting." Ashley bounced on her toes as she clapped her hands. "You brought your little friend with you." Ashley bent down to welcome Montgomery, and he bounded up to her. "Would you like a little puppy treat? Sure you do. Let me get you something special." She turned and stepped into her storage room, returning with something cupped in her hand. Montgomery smelled it right away. He looked up at her with expectation, his tail thumping on the floor. Ashley held out her hand to him and opened it. Montgomery lunged forward and lapped up his treat.

When Ashley looked up, Emma explained. "They arrested Barney this morning, and we're finally rid of him."

"About time," Ashley said. "Oops. Shouldn't have said that. Pretend you didn't hear it."

"The last thing he said before they hauled him away," Emma said, "was 'Attend to Montgomery. He's all I have left.' So I now have a dog to care for. I figured you'd be the best person to help me. Do you have a leash I can borrow?"

"Certainly." Ashley ducked into the room and returned with her bag of doggy things. She pulled out a leash and handed it to Emma. She reached back in. "And you'll need these too."

"What are they?"

"Poop bags, of course."

Emma rolled her eyes. "Great."

Ashley rummaged through the bag. "Here's a longer leash too. You can keep everything. I won't be needing them."

"Why?" Emma asked. "I thought you wanted a dog."

"I did. But now it doesn't seem so important. When Topher and I get married, we want to start our family right away. A dog won't get much attention if we have a baby to care for."

Even though the cosmetologist was four years older, Emma viewed Ashley as a peer. The thought of her friend having a baby jarred her. Yet when she and Joshua got married, they might make the same decision. She shuddered at the thought.

Ashley pulled out a toy from the bag and squeaked it twice, tossing it into the corner of her shop. That's when Emma noticed the doggy bed still there in the corner. Montgomery bounded toward the squeaky toy, grabbed it in his mouth, and retreated to the bed. He snuggled down, his eyes darting between Emma and Ashley, as if waiting for one of them to say something.

"Be sure to keep him hydrated," Ashley said. "If you're thirsty, he probably is too. And make sure he doesn't get overheated. When I'm done working, I'll help you get set up for tonight. I should have every-thing you need—I know I do. Even dog food."

Emma crouched to clip the short leash on Montgomery's collar. When she stood, he darted around her and stood at her right side.

Ashley's eyes sparkled. "Looks like someone's been to puppy school. You should check into that. Half of puppy school is training the owner."

The weight of being a puppy parent was looming large. So much responsibility. Emma wondered if she was ready for it.

Ashley agreed to meet Emma at her room shortly after five. Emma turned to leave.

"Tell him to heel," Ashley called out. "Say it with authority."

"Heel, Montgomery!" The puppy scooted up to Emma and walked along on her right side, his head held high and his tail wagging.

Emma held her head high, too, a pleased grin plastered on her face.

Her phone vibrated. She had a text. It wasn't anyone on her contact list. Puzzled, she read the message aloud, as if Montgomery needed to hear it. "It's time for us to meet. Since you can't drive, I'll come to you. This Thursday at 3:00. —PM."

Who in the world is PM?

2: DOGGIE BEDS

Emma forwarded the mysterious text message to Hernandez, the head of security, and asked if he could track down who sent it. Then she tried to push this new worry from her mind. She asked the Sovereign for help to do just that.

After Emma wrapped up her workday, she and Montgomery met Ashley at her room in the priests' quarters. Ashley shared the essentials of caring for a puppy. They discussed food, exercise, and grooming. She gave Emma a food dish that matched the water bowl.

But as Ashley surveyed Emma's tiny room, she shook her head. "There's barely enough space for you. His bowls hardly fit. The only place for his doggie bed is in front of the door. You could trip over it in the dark as you go to turn on the light. What would you think about him sleeping with you?"

"In my bed?" Emma squirmed. "Is it sanitary? Safe? Seems a bit strange."

"Non-dog people often think so," Ashley answered, "but most owners embrace the idea. And their dogs like it too."

"Why?"

"They're pack animals and view their owners as part of their pack, often even the alpha dog. Sleeping together reinforces their bond. It also comforts them and helps them feel secure. And if they're cold, they snuggle next to their owners to keep warm. Give it a try. Once you get used to it, you'll probably like it too."

Emma still wasn't sure about it. It somehow felt wrong. Emma always tried to seek the Sovereign about spiritual matters, but not so much about other things. Yet anything that troubled her should be worth talking about with the Sovereign. As silly as it seemed, Emma did just that. She prayed silently in her spirit. *Is it okay for me to let Montgomery sleep in my bed with me?*

The Sovereign's gentle laugh echoed in Emma's

head. *Of course it is! But thanks for asking. You should never hesitate to talk to me about anything that concerns you.*

Emma turned to Ashley. "I'll consider it."

"Let's try an experiment," the cosmetologist said. "I'll leave his doggie bed here, and you let him decide where he wants to sleep. I expect he'll pick your bed."

Emma agreed to Ashley's little test. Then, under her instructor's watchful eye, Emma refilled Montgomery's water bowl. Next, she opened a can of dog food and spooned it into the matching dish.

Appreciative for Ashley's doggie advice and pet supplies, Emma wrapped her arms around her friend. "Thanks for all your help in getting me started." They walked from her room in the priests' quarters and out the exterior doors on the lower level.

Scarlett Steele from Xtend News Network stood there, along with her cameraman. Emma had completely forgotten about their interview.

3: TOURING THE TEMPLE

As Ashley walked away, the smiling reporter strode forward. "I appreciate your willingness to give us a tour of the Temple grounds," Scarlett said. "But why did you want to start with the priests' quarters?"

Emma shrugged. "This was just a good place to meet. There's nothing interesting to see."

"But since we're here," Scarlett said, "let's tour it anyway—unless it's off-limits. You narrate, and I'll edit as needed. I can even change the order of the tour to make for a more interesting piece."

Though Emma hadn't intended to let Scarlett see her quarters, she had nothing to hide or be ashamed about. Emma opened the exterior door to the priests' quarters for them to enter. The cameraman stepped in front of Scarlett and sped in. Then he spun around to video the two of them walking in, along with Montgomery.

"We may as well start with my room." Emma gestured to her right. She turned the knob and let the door swing into the room, but she didn't enter. There was no way the three of them would fit.

Scarlett peered in. "Oh, my! It's so small. I assumed you lived in the High Priest's residence in the palace." Scarlett stepped back and waved for the cameraman to step forward. Standing in the doorway, he panned the room from left to right, top to bottom. It didn't take long.

"At first, I stayed in the High Priest's quarters, but it didn't feel right," Emma said. "I'm a simple girl, and it was too fancy. If this is good enough for the priests, it's good enough for me."

"Are all the priests' rooms like this?" Scarlett asked.

Emma shook her head. "I understand my room, and the one across the hall, are a bit smaller than the rest of them on this floor. But as the only room available, I'm glad to take it. The rest of the rooms on this floor are small and dated. I hope we'll soon be able to spruce them up a bit."

Emma led the tour up the stairs to the second floor. "Since the quarters are built into the side of a hill, each floor is larger than the one below it. On this level, the rooms are about twice the size and up to date. The third-floor rooms are even bigger and nicely furnished. But for the priests' privacy, I can't show you any rooms. Sorry."

"Understood," Scarlett said. "Where next?"

"I'll take you on the most efficient route," Emma said. "The palace is next."

Emma guided the tour to the back entrance of the palace. She showed them her office, the small meeting area next to it, and the conference room.

"Is this where you hold staff meetings?" Scarlett asked.

Emma shook her head. "Staff meetings are a waste of time, but I do have a working lunch with my team every weekday. We cover all the important stuff there."

Emma gestured toward Frederick's office and Mark's. "These are the offices for our executive administrator and our Chief of Priests." Emma also showed Scarlett the banquet hall, dining room, and grand foyer. Then she took them to the High Priest's residence. "It's larger than a small house and has much more space than I need. Right now we can't use it because we must replace some piping that has lead in it."

"Will you move back here once that's resolved?" Scarlett asked.

Emma shook her head. "It's not right for me, but I suspect we'll have some special uses for it in the future."

Emma guided the tour to the new auditorium. "Those who watch our services online have already seen most of it. But let me show you some behind-the-scenes areas." They peeked into the sound booth and the control room, viewed one of the small meeting spaces on the periphery, and ended at Emma's dressing room behind the stage.

"Why is yours last?" Scarlett asked. "I think you should have the one that's closest and biggest."

"The first one is for the main officiant of the service. Next is for any guest speaker we may have. The last one is fine for me. It's where I change into my robe and make final preparations. Mostly I pray for the service."

Emma opened the door, and they walked inside. There hung Emma's new robe, the pink one the Sovereign had suggested she get. Apparently, the tailor had finished it and left it as a surprise.

Scarlett gushed. "It's beautiful."

"There's nothing in the Holy Text that says what color a robe should be," Emma said. "I think pink is better for me than dingy earth tones or even the light blue one I've worn lately. Want a sneak peek?"

Emma took the robe off the hanger and shimmied into it. She stretched her arms out to her sides and beamed. "Ta-da!"

"It fits perfectly," Scarlett said.

"I had no doubt," Emma answered. "Our tailor is the best."

Emma removed the robe and placed it back on the hanger, ready for Sunday. She led the tour outside. "The ancient Temple is next." With care, the trio approached a bustle of construction workers. "Normally, it's open for visitors and tours, but this week we're making some updates to bring it up to code and do some maintenance. They're working around the clock to get it done as quickly as possible. When it reopens, we'll reinstate the daily prayer times we read about in the Holy Text—three times each day. We also plan to hold an ancient service on Sundays. We'll attempt to mirror exactly what the Holy Text says."

"I thought that's what you were doing for services in the new auditorium," Scarlett said.

"In the new auditorium, we're following the practices we read about in Scripture, but we adapt them to align with today's culture. For example, the ancients used the common instruments of their day. Our modern-day instruments are guitars and drums. That's what we use in the services in the new auditorium." Emma paused to make sure she wasn't covering things too fast.

"For the ancient services in the old Temple, we'll attempt to do exactly what the Holy Text says —to the degree possible. After all, who knows what a seven-and-a-half-stringed goticature is? Even so, it should be a spiritually insightful experience."

Waving to Ezra as they walked past the ancient Temple, Emma guided their trio to the old auditorium. "As you know, we're now offering traditional services here. It focuses on organ music and choirs. Gavin is heading that up. Our soft launch last Sunday was a success."

Scarlett frowned. "Are organs in Scripture?"

"Great question," Emma said. "It's more cultural than anything, but it's what some people need to better worship the Sovereign and pursue their faith."

The school was next. Emma talked about the microschool her teacher, Jennifer, had set up for her and her disciples. "We're working on reopening the Temple school to train future priests," Emma told Scarlett. "For the first batch, it will need to be people who live locally, because the dorm rooms need a lot of work to get them usable. Later, people from across the country—and around the world—can apply."

"Will it be just men?" Scarlett asked. "Or will your reforms focus on training women priests?"

Emma smiled. "I appreciate you asking. We can't fix past discrimination by replacing it with a different form of discrimination. That'd be even worse because it's intentional. When we reopen, the Temple school will take applications from anyone who wants to become a priest. We'll pick the applicants by merit, not gender."

Emma guided the tour through the library, support buildings—which included the clinic her father ran—and administration. They ended at the cafeteria, just as it was getting dusk. "I have some ideas for updating the cafeteria too," Emma said. "But since I haven't talked to anyone about them— and we already have too many projects going on—I shouldn't share my ideas now. But you'll be the first to know when the time comes."

"You already mentioned several projects," Scarlett said. "Are there others?"

Emma began counting on her fingers. "First, we have the work on the ancient Temple. There are also some repairs to be made in the old auditorium, but they're minor. We have the lead problem to resolve in the palace. And the bigger project is getting the dorms ready to use again. I didn't mention it, but Ezra is working on plans to build a welcome center next to the Temple. I'm really excited about that." Emma scrunched up her face. "I think I'm forgetting something, but, anyway, we have a lot going on."

"All these projects sound expensive," Scarlett said. "How are you going to pay for them? Will you hold a fundraiser?"

Emma smiled. "Though we struggled with finances in the past, right now things are good. Weekly donations are up, and we had several recent onetime developments that brought in a lot of money. We've allocated those funds for these projects. So we're all set."

Throughout the tour, Montgomery had

behaved himself well, and Emma mostly forgot about him trotting at her side. But then he squatted.

"Montgomery!" Emma yelled. "Stop!"

He didn't.

The cameraman caught it all.

That's when Emma realized she had left the poop bags back in her room.

4: CHANGED MY LIFE

Emma's eyes popped open in horror. Scarlett laughed. So did the cameraman.

In a panic, Emma shoved Montgomery's leash at Scarlett. "Watch him for a moment. Be right back." She spun around and dashed to her room. Fortunately, it was close. Within seconds, she returned, panting, with poop bag in hand. But she had never used one. Studying it, she tried to figure out how to get the poop into it.

Scarlett laughed again. "Slide your hand into it like a glove. Then pick up the poop."

Emma did as instructed. It smelled so bad. She gagged and thought she might puke.

"Now pull the opening of the bag over it. Knot the top to tie it shut. And toss it. Easy peasy."

Emma survived the ordeal. Barely. Lightheaded and queasy, she took Montgomery's leash back from Scarlett. "Sorry. It's my first day being a puppy parent. I have so much to learn."

Scarlett cocked her head and peered at Emma. "Is this Barney Clark's dog? The one that was with you when you freed the prisoners?"

"It is. He asked me to take care of Montgomery when he was arrested."

"Wait just a second," Scarlett interjected. "You mean you're watching the dog of the man accused of trying to kill you?"

Emma nodded. "It seems like the right thing to do."

Scarlett shook her head. "You provide a remarkable example for all to follow."

"Any credit belongs to the Sovereign."

"I have a follow up question from our tour," Scarlett said. "We covered every building except this one next to the cafeteria." The reporter pointed to her right. "What's it used for?"

"At the moment, nothing," Emma said. "But it's part of my plans that I'm not ready to talk about yet."

As the three of them headed to the front of the Temple grounds to the network news van, Emma turned to Scarlett. "I know you're in town to visit your parents. How much longer will you be here?"

"I'm staying," Scarlett said. "They reassigned me to cover this area, specifically focusing on you and all the activity here on the Temple grounds."

"How exciting!" The news pleased Emma. "Does that mean I can look forward to more interviews with you in the future?"

"Most assuredly. You changed my life, and I'll never be able to repay you."

"The Sovereign changed your life," Emma corrected. "I was just the conduit."

"From a spiritual standpoint, I agree. But you also changed my career. I give you full credit for that. Before our first interview, I was a struggling reporter trying to make a name for myself. And I was failing. They had me on probation. Then Barney got me fired. But you intervened, and I got a second chance."

"It was the right thing to do," Emma said.

"The second interview we did after you freed the prisoners was, at the time, the top watched broadcast of our network—ever. That got everyone's attention."

"What do you mean *at the time*?"

"Our follow-up interview about Joshua's resurrection from the dead far surpassed it. In fact, every interview I've done with you since then has landed in our top ten most watched shows. They view me as their 'golden girl' and the reason our viewership is up.

"They moved me here to cover you and all Temple activity for broadcast reporting, to write articles for our website, and to pursue investigative journalism, which is what I trained to do."

"What's investigative journalism?" Emma asked.

"It's doing deep research into a serious crime, injustice, or political corruption. It can take weeks or even months of work. But they've given me the latitude to pursue it if something interesting comes up—providing I don't let my other responsibilities slide."

The trio reached the news van, and the cameraman stowed his gear. Scarlett gave Emma an emotional hug. "Again, thank you for changing my life. I'll never forget it." She got in the van and left.

As the van disappeared, Hernandez squealed into the parking lot and screeched to a stop in front of Emma.

Emma's heart thumped, and she held her breath, panicked over Hernandez's breakneck arrival and worried over the news he would deliver.

5: SECRET IDENTITIES

A flustered Hernandez jumped out of his car and rushed to Emma. "Sorry I didn't get here sooner, but you didn't reply to my texts. I wanted to warn you to be on your guard around Scarlett Steele. She isn't who she says she is. Don't trust her for a second."

Emma studied the man's normally reserved face. He seemed worked up about something, but his concern over Scarlett made no sense. "Why?"

"I've been digging into her and can't find anything about her prior to her employment with Xtend News Network. It's like she didn't exist before then. There's no record of her attending Riverside High like she claimed. Nor is there any

record of her going to college or earning a journalism degree. She's as phony as can be. I can't
figure out what she's up to, but when I do, she'll be
out of here for good."

Emma let out the breath that she'd been hold-
ing. She brought her hand to her chin. "I'm sure
there's some mistake. I trust her and don't sense any
pretense in her spirit."

"But how can you explain that she didn't exist
prior to three years ago?"

Emma shook her head but then brightened with
an idea. "She said she had Mrs. Butler for religion
class in high school. Let's check with her."

"I'll do that first thing tomorrow," Hernandez
said.

"Or we can ask her tonight," Emma countered.
"I'm sure she's still working. Let's head to the
Temple school building."

Hernandez shook his head. "There's nothing
she could say to ease my concerns, but for your
sake, I'm willing to listen."

The pair headed to the Temple school building.
Hernandez's allegations against Scarlett battled
Emma's own perception of the reporter.

Hernandez interrupted her thoughts. "I also
found out who sent you the mysterious text."

Emma slowed her pace and turned to look at her head of security. "Who?"

"PM isn't someone's initials. It's their title. I suspected PM might stand for Prime Minister and verified it."

"Seriously? How did you find out?"

"I visited Barney Clark in prison—"

"Why would you do that?" Emma snapped. "Surely there were other ways to find out without asking him."

"You're right, but he was my best option for a speedy answer. He also identified the number as the Prime Minister's personal cell phone. Apparently, he had used it often to communicate with her."

"I wonder why she wants to talk to me?"

"I don't know," Hernandez said, "but I suspect Barney does, though he wouldn't tell me. He insisted on speaking to you directly. I informed him that wasn't an option, and he said that going forward, he will only communicate personally with you."

Worry covered Emma's face. "Do I have to see him?" As far as she was concerned—good aide or not—she never wanted to see that evil man again. "Please don't make me!"

"Of course not. I'll look for other ways to

uncover what he knows. You have nothing to worry about as far as Barney Clark is concerned."

They walked in silence the rest of the way to the Temple school building. They found Mrs. Butler easily enough. She was getting the second classroom ready for school. Her former teacher brightened when she saw Emma, but her smile faded when she glimpsed Hernandez. "This doesn't look like a social call. What's up?"

Hernandez sucked in a slow breath, but Emma spoke first. "Hernandez tried to investigate Scarlett Steele but can't find anything about her prior to her working at her present job. There's not even a record of her going to college or attending Riverside High. But she said she took your classes when she was there. Is that right?"

Mrs. Butler's frame relaxed. A pleased gleam formed. "She was indeed my student. But Scarlett Steele is her professional name. So her school records will give her birth name. As soon as you hear it, you'll realize why she changed it—for the sake of her career." Mrs. Butler's gaze flitted from Emma to Hernandez and back to Emma. Her eyes sparkled. She was clearly enjoying the building tension.

"Don't keep us in suspense," Hernandez bellowed.

"Investigate her birth name," Mrs. Butler said. "It's Gertrude Scarborough."

6: GUITARS VERSUS PIPE ORGAN

Emma strode to her room, still snickering that Scarlett Steele's real name was Gertrude Scarborough. Just thinking about it made her chuckle.

It had been a full day. It started with the arrest of Barney Clark. His departure led to a puppy to care for. Later there was a successful interview with Scarlett. The revelation that the Prime Minister was behind the strange text message solved another mystery, but it filled Emma with worry.

It was now late in the day and Emma had missed supper. The cafeteria was closed. She wouldn't be able to eat until breakfast. Her stomach rumbled with discontent. That's when she realized she was a bit lightheaded too.

She flipped on the light in her room. A surprise awaited her. On her tiny desk sat a tray of food, along with a note. "Thought you might be hungry. Prayed for your interview. Love, Ashley."

Though Emma wanted to scarf the food, Montgomery came first. She put fresh water in his bowl and gave him a quick brushing. Then she ate her meal as she studied the Holy Text. She had never eaten while exploring Scripture, and it didn't feel quite right. But she didn't want to cut her study time short and knew she must eat.

The only way to do both was to do them at the same time. She wasn't sure if the Sovereign would approve of this compromise or not, yet Emma also didn't ask.

She finished her meal and licked her fingers as she made her last journal entry. It was a few minutes after 10:00, a deadline she seldom pushed past. She took Montgomery out for a quick walk. He peed right away and then wanted to go back inside. She was glad. Removing his leash, she coaxed him into his doggie bed, flicked off the light, and shuffled to bed.

Emma closed her eyes and was just nicely settled when he bounded up to join her. She ruffled the hair on his head and scratched under his chin.

A sigh leaked out of the contented puppy. He spun around and shimmied down to a comfortable spot, with his butt facing her and his wagging tail fanning her face.

With an amused smile, Emma thanked the Sovereign for all that had happened during the day. As she sought the Sovereign's blessing for tomorrow, she fell asleep mid-thought.

Emma awoke the next morning with more energy than usual. Thanking the Sovereign for the new day and all its potential, Emma edged off the bed without disturbing Montgomery. Yet when she flicked on the light, the tiny pup's head jerked up, eyes wide open.

She readied for the day and joined the priests for breakfast. Montgomery's presence distracted them, but they were attentive to what Emma wanted to share. "After we meet at two to discuss the Holy Text, I'm meeting with Jennifer at three to plan for reopening the Temple school to train future priests. Anyone who wants to can join us. Also, please let me know the seminaries you attended and if it prepared you for your work here."

Emma blessed them for the day and hustled off to school. She had a question for Jennifer before class started.

When all of Emma's twelve disciples arrived, Jennifer opened the day with prayer and invited Emma forward.

"Today I'd like to start a new practice," Emma announced. "We'll take a few minutes each Wednesday morning to talk about what we need to do to help prepare you to become priests. Think about what area you'd like to focus on. If you don't know, that's okay. But if you do, we can move you in that direction."

When Emma returned to her seat, Montgomery wasn't there. She scanned the room in a panic. Then she spotted him huddled down in the back corner of the room, right where Barney used to sit. *That must be his spot.*

School went well that morning. She and Joshua finished first and had about an hour together before lunch. She hadn't spent much time with him lately, but he understood. He was patient. That was just one more reason why she loved him. They strolled the Temple grounds, hand in hand, discussing their future.

"Would you like to go on a date?" Emma asked.

"That's my plan," Joshua said. "Just as soon as I can drive and get a car."

"I was thinking sooner. What about tonight?"

"Unless our date is in the cafeteria, I'm not sure how you'll pull that off."

Emma gazed up into her boyfriend's beautiful brown eyes. "Jennifer invited us to go on a double date with her and her boyfriend, David."

"A double date, huh? I've never been on one."

"Neither of us have. Not even a regular date. I know it's last minute but tonight will work for the rest of us. What about you?"

Joshua slowed his pace and then stopped. He stared across the pond. "I think that works. I'll text Mom."

Emma pulled out her phone. "And I'll text Jennifer. We'll leave at five to meet David at the restaurant."

"On second thought," Joshua said, "that won't work. Though I have money in the bank, I don't know how to get it out to pay for our meal."

"Same with me, but Jennifer said it's their treat."

"I suppose that'd be okay for just this once." Joshua let go of Emma's hand and wrapped his arm around her back, pulling her close. She tipped her head into his shoulder and sighed.

They strolled along in silence.

Emma entertained happy thoughts about their

future together, but Joshua's mind apparently went elsewhere. "I'd like to work with Gavin in the old sanctuary," he said, "and help with the traditional service."

Emma recoiled at his revelation, turning to face him. "Seriously? Pipe organ music?" She envisioned them working together, ministering side-by-side, in the contemporary service. But she stopped herself from voicing her opinion. She'd already learned that for their relationship to work, she couldn't tell him what to do—even though she was the High Priestess. Not only was it wrong, but it was also disrespectful.

"My parents like pipe organ music and listen to it at home—all the time. It's what my sister and I are used to hearing. It helps us connect with the Sovereign."

Adjusting her perspective, Emma reached for his hand and smiled. "I'm excited for you to work there and see what the Sovereign will accomplish through you."

"I know that's not what you wanted to hear, but thanks for supporting me." Joshua gave her hand a quick squeeze. "You like guitars, and I like pipe organs."

Emma squeezed his hand back. "And thank you

for being patient with me as I learn how to be a better girlfriend."

They arrived at the cafeteria just before noon. After getting their food, Joshua retreated to the table where Emma's disciples normally sat. She headed to the table where her team met for lunch. The focus of the day's discussion was on the ancient Temple's repairs.

"Each of the construction trades has made this project a priority." Ezra beamed. "They want to do what they can to support our work here. They're working around the clock to finish fast. The goal is to reopen by next Monday. I got the same response from our architect, who will have her initial welcome center proposal to us this Friday."

Emma shared that she and Jennifer would meet with some priests that afternoon to discuss details of the Temple school. What she didn't mention, however, was her concern over tomorrow's meeting with the Prime Minister.

7: THE DEBACLE

Emma met with the priests after lunch to talk about the Holy Text. They covered Prophecy chapter 47 and most of 48. After Emma first proposed a daily discussion, she soon realized she knew more about the Holy Text than any of them. Though she'd only been studying it for a few months, they had never read it at all—until she arrived.

Their discussion became more like her teaching and them asking questions or adding an occasional thought. Even Gabe—though well-versed in Scripture—never said much. Emma wasn't sure if he didn't want to talk or was giving her space to lead. Yet when he did share, his insights were both wise and helpful.

As their hour together neared its end, Emma repeated what she had told them that morning. "Anyone who wants to help plan for reopening the Temple school can join Jennifer and me. Though I need to leave for that meeting, please keep discussing Prophecy chapter 48."

She knew they probably wouldn't, but prayed that one day they would continue without her there to lead them. On the days when she couldn't join them, she understood they'd meet for a few minutes and then give up. At least that's what Mark had told her.

When Emma left, a few priests followed her. Mark moved up to walk next to her. "Each of the priests wanted to join us, but we realized that would be too many so we appointed six representatives. I also have a list of all the seminaries they attended and can confirm that no one felt their education prepared them to serve here at the Temple—at least not with the reforms you're making. They all agree that you've helped them more in the past few weeks than in their three years of advanced education. Though they learned much there, little of it applies here."

"That's what I thought," Emma said. "Thanks for confirming. Will you be at the meeting? Along with Jennifer, that will make nine. The conference room in the palace will be a better place to meet than the auditorium."

"An excellent idea," Mark said. "I'll text Jennifer about the change in venue." Then the pair led their troupe past the new auditorium and headed to the palace.

With everyone gathered around the conference table, Emma prayed. She asked the Sovereign to bless their meeting and guide their discussion.

Emma and Jennifer had already talked about what they envisioned and agreed on the direction. But they wanted input from the priests to round out their plans and spot any areas they had overlooked.

Jennifer began the discussion. "I view the microschool we started as the precursor for reopening the Temple school. We'll cover all required high school material, focus on studying the Holy Text, and provide work opportunities so students can apply what they've learned and explore various functions here on the Temple grounds."

"We're completely against training high schoolers to be priests," Mark said. "If we open that door, then anyone would think they could become a priest."

"What's wrong with that?" Emma snapped. "I'm in high school. The same with my twelve friends. I'm already in the priest role, and my friends are moving toward it."

"You're the exception," Mark said. "And we're making allowances for your so-called disciples in deference to you. But none of us want to see this pattern continue."

"We must maintain the prestige of the priest-hood," said the priest on Mark's right.

"So true," said the priest on Mark's left. "We invested a lot of time and money to earn our credentials. Don't cheapen our preparation by letting teenagers become priests."

Emma jumped up and stared down at the priests. She planted her knuckles on the table and glared at them as she leaned forward.

When Jennifer placed a gentle hand on Emma's forearm, she lowered her frame back to her seat, saying a silent prayer. *Help me, Sovereign. Give me the right words.*

Yet the Sovereign remained silent, which Emma took as a sign for her to stay silent as well.

"By your own admissions," Jennifer said, "your seminary education did nothing to prepare you for the actual work here at the Temple. Why do you want to force others to follow that same unproductive path?"

The priest on Mark's right leaned forward and slapped his hand on the table. The priest to Mark's left began to stand. Mark placed a hand on them both, and they withdrew. He cleared his throat. "Our fear is that adults will not respond well to teenagers being priests. We're only thinking about what's best for all concerned."

"But they respect me," Emma said. "Most everyone here treats me as an adult. The only people who didn't are the ones who resist change—and they're no longer here."

"Keep in mind," Jennifer said, "that our high schoolers training to become priests will not have any public-facing roles until they graduate and are, in fact, adults. I don't see it as a problem."

"I do!" Mark jumped to his feet. "In all due respect to the High Priestess, I see it as a tremendous problem."

"Perhaps it's best that we adjourn," Jennifer said, "and reconvene later with cooler heads."

"I concur." Mark marched from the room. The other six priests stomped out behind him.

Emma and Jennifer remained seated. The shocked High Priestess shook her head and cast a questioning glance at her teacher. "What just happened? I don't think that could've gone any worse."

"It could have indeed been much worse," Jennifer corrected. "It's just that neither one of us expected conflict. We need to be aware of that potential in the future. It's clear that you and I have one vision, and the priests have a different one."

That's when the Sovereign answered Emma's prayer. That's when Emma found clarity. At last she knew what to say. "We have two needs to fill with our Temple school. One track is a high school curriculum to prepare graduates to become priests. The other is to train adults—those who've already completed high school and maybe even college. It should cover both those who have been to seminary and those who haven't. There is not one plan to make, but two."

"I agree with Emma," came Mark's voice from behind.

Jennifer and Emma turned to see the remorseful priest standing in the doorway. "I apologize for my role in this conflict and for not guiding the priests in a more productive manner. Emma has succinctly summarized our dilemma and showed us the way forward." Mark moved into the room and returned to his original spot at the table. "Shall we get started? Or, more correctly, shall we get restarted?"

Jennifer nodded. "We're ready."

Emma corralled her hair and moved it behind her shoulders, cooling the back of her neck. "We shared our plans to train high schoolers to become priests after they graduate. If we address the priests' concerns, can we start our high school track next school year?"

As Emma spoke, the two priests who had voiced their frustration also returned and sat next to Mark. "I apologize for losing my temper," said the priest on Mark's right. "My hand still smarts." Sheepishly, he held up a red palm. "Knowing that you've heard us and will address our concerns is all the assurance I need."

The priest's counterpart on Mark's left nodded.

"As far as training adults for the priesthood," Emma said, "I think the focus should be on studying the Holy Text."

"I concur," Mark said. The two priests flanking him also agreed.

"Having them retake high school classes makes no sense," Emma said, "but we must be clear that their seminary training fell short. We also don't want to make people go to seminary first. That makes no sense either. What if we did an eighteen-month advanced course focusing on the Holy Text and how to apply it? They could spend half their day studying and the other half experiencing various jobs here at the Temple. Then I think they'd be ready."

While Emma talked, the other four priests had slunk back into the room, respectfully returning to their original seats.

"I wonder if we could complete it in twelve months instead of eighteen?" Mark asked. The other priests murmured their agreement.

"Why don't we make that our tentative plan," Jennifer said. "But before we finalize it, I'd like to talk with Elizabeth Butler to get her input, as she'll be the primary one teaching the Holy Text."

Everyone smiled and stood. Mark shook Jennifer's hand and then Emma's. The other priests all did the same thing. Emma still didn't understand this handshaking ritual, but she knew it was an important gesture for many adults.

She still had a lot to learn.

She also had a date to get ready for.

8: MORE THAN A DATE

Though the meeting with the priests ended well, it went much later than Emma expected. Rushing back to her room to get ready for her date, she only had time to wash her face, change clothes, and brush her hair.

After feeding Montgomery and telling him she'd be back in a couple of hours, Emma dashed out the door of her room and bumped into Joshua.

"I thought I'd pick you up for our date," he said with a wink and a smirk.

"How romantic!" Emma winked back.

They hustled to meet Jennifer at her car, where their teacher awaited them. Joshua opened the passenger door for Emma and gestured for her to get in.

"Why don't you sit up front?" Emma said to Joshua as she opened the rear door and climbed into the back.

Jennifer turned to look at Emma. "I've informed David that, contrary to what he was taught, he is not to kneel, bow, or call you 'My Lord.' I also told him that eye contact is permissible—even preferred."

"Thanks," Emma said. "Though I finally stopped everyone at the Temple grounds from doing these things, I forgot it could still happen when I'm in public."

"Hopefully it won't tonight," Jennifer said. "We're going to a quaint little diner that David and I like. Their food is fantastic. Given that it's early on a Wednesday evening, it shouldn't be busy at all."

"Thanks for inviting us on a double date," Emma said. "We really appreciate it."

"For sure." Joshua looked at Jennifer but squirmed.

"There's no need to be nervous," Jennifer said as she drove toward the diner. "You see me every day."

"*Then* you're my teacher," Joshua said. "This is different."

"When we're not in school, I hope you can

think of me as a friend. That's what Emma does, and we get on just fine."

To break the tense silence that followed, Emma updated Joshua on how the Temple school meeting with the priests ended. But she left out the drama from the first half.

"When my sister is old enough," Joshua said, "I think she'd like to go to school here and become a priest too."

"I wonder the same thing about the sibs," Emma said. "I think Hailey would like it, but I'm not sure about Brayden. He has a crush on your sister, though, so that could tip his decision."

Then Emma turned to Jennifer. "Hailey and Brayden are twins. They're in the same grade as Joshua's sister, Sarah. They're three years younger than us, so we'll have graduated by the time they show up—assuming they decide to attend."

"One thing we haven't discussed," Jennifer said, "is how we'll select applicants." She turned the car into the diner's lot and parked. "It looks like David's already here. I can't wait for you to meet him."

Already sitting in a booth, David stood and waved to Jennifer as they entered the diner. She slid in next to him. Joshua sat across from him, and

Emma slid in last. They had just finished introductions when the waitress hustled over.

"Hi," she said with a wide smile. "My name is Zoe, and I'll be taking care of you tonight. Would you like a beverage to get started?" She scanned the group, starting with Jennifer, working around the table, and ending with Emma.

Zoe gasped. "Oh, my! Are you . . . are you Emma Barlow? I mean the High Priestess? Oh my. You are! I'm totally freaking out. My apologies." She tipped her head down and then kneeled. "I'm happy to serve you, My Lord."

Emma laid her hand on Zoe's arm. "Please call me Emma and treat me like everyone else. I'd be honored if you think of me as your new friend and not the High Priestess."

By now, everyone in the diner was staring at the kneeling Zoe. Their gaze then moved to Emma, but they quickly looked away and began whispering among themselves.

Emma took Zoe's outstretched hand and lifted it. "Please stand. It's okay."

Zoe stood, straightened her frame, and adjusted her apron. She brushed the hair from her face, touched the three piercings on her left eyebrow, and lowered her hand to cover the tattoo on her forearm. "I apologize for my appearance. And for not wearing a clean uniform."

"No worries," Emma said. "I hear your food is fantastic. What do you recommend?"

Zoe relaxed her tense body. "My favorite is the grilled cheese . . . but maybe the deluxe steak burger basket would be more appropriate for you. It's the most expensive thing on the menu."

"Grilled cheese would be perfect," Emma said.

Zoe jotted this and the other three orders on her notepad. "I'll get this in right away and put a rush on it." Zoe executed a cute little curtsy, spun around, and dashed away.

Their food soon arrived and was as good as Jennifer had said. They savored their meal and enjoyed their conversation.

Emma studied David and Jennifer. They seemed like a perfect couple. She was so happy for the small part she had played in getting them reconnected.

Though their food was gone, their conversation continued. After an hour, the diner was packed. It seemed no one was leaving. "I suggest we vamoose to free up space," David said. He waved at Zoe and beckoned her. "When you have a moment, please give us our check. Then we can open this table for other guests."

"Tonight's meals are on the house," Zoe said. "We're honored at the High Priestess's presence at our humble diner."

"We appreciate your generous offer," David said, "but we insist on paying for our food."

When Zoe glanced at Emma, the High Priestess nodded her agreement.

Zoe pulled a completed check from her apron pocket, crossed off the words *on the house*, and handed it to David.

"Thank you," he said. "We appreciate your fine food and excellent service."

Emma pulled out her phone and handed it to Zoe. "Will you take a picture of the four of us? It's an important night I want to remember. It's also our first date." Emma tipped her head toward Joshua.

"I was wondering." Zoe glowed. "I'm so stoked your first date was here at our little diner. I'll never forget tonight."

After taking a picture of all four of them, Zoe zoomed in and took a couple more shots of Emma and Joshua, who slid up to Emma and put his arm around her shoulder.

Zoe looked at the last shot. "Perfect!" She handed the phone back to Emma.

The four of them stood to leave. That's when Zoe pulled out her phone. "If it's not too much to ask, can I take a picture of you?"

As David and Jennifer went to the cashier to pay for dinner, Zoe snapped a couple of shots of Emma and Joshua, along with several of just Emma.

"Would you like a picture of the two of us?" Emma asked Zoe.

Their waitress's face beamed as she handed her phone to Joshua. "Do you mind?"

Joshua took a half a dozen pictures and gave the phone back.

"And maybe your autograph too?"

This was Emma's first request for an autograph since becoming High Priestess, but it wasn't an unfamiliar experience. After some of the plays she starred in, especially the musicals where she had the lead, people would sometimes ask for her autograph.

Though as High Priestess, the request troubled her, Emma willingly complied. Below her signature, she added a Scripture reference: Wisdom 7.241.

"What does the verse say?" Zoe asked. "I'm still

reading the History section and haven't gotten to Wisdom yet."

"It ends with 'the words of a true friend heal, restore, and strengthen.' I view you as a friend."

Zoe's lower lip quivered, and her eyelids fluttered. She opened her mouth, but no words came out. *Thank you,* she mouthed.

One patron timidly approached and asked for a picture and autograph. Soon a line formed. Emma spent the next twenty minutes posing for pictures, giving hugs, and autographing everything people shoved in front of her.

The whole time, Joshua stood by her side, giving her support and ready to intervene if needed. Grateful for his patience, Emma prayed that the attention she was receiving wasn't irritating David and Jennifer or ruining their evening.

But when it came time to leave, they were nowhere in sight.

9: QUESTIONS

Confused, Emma and Joshua walked outside the diner. Her heart pounded in a panic. "Lord," she prayed, "show us what to do."

"Last I noticed, they were standing right here," Joshua said. "Would they ditch us?"

Emma shook her head. "But where are they? Jennifer's car is gone."

"Emma! Joshua! Over here."

Jennifer waved at them from the other side of the parking lot, standing next to a fancy sports car.

Relieved, they hustled over to her.

"Sorry for the confusion," Jennifer apologized. "David had an emergency at work and had to leave right away. But he didn't have enough gas in his car. He'd planned to fill up after dinner. I told him to take mine instead. He refused, but I insisted. Though once he left, I didn't feel comfortable waiting outside by myself, so I retreated to his car."

Joshua scowled. "So he left us with a car that has no gas?"

"Don't worry. There's a station down the street." Jennifer pointed to her right. "We're fine. It's just that he didn't have enough gas to drive straight to work."

This time Joshua insisted Emma sit in the front. He folded his lanky frame into the back. "I've always wanted to ride in a sports car," he said as he situated himself.

"Sorry for the tight fit back there," Jennifer said.

"No problem." Joshua made a quarter turn and stretched his legs out onto the seat. Then he awkwardly managed to belt himself in. "Good to go."

Jennifer roared the car to life. Though the throaty engine begged her to go fast, she putzed to the gas station. After filling the tank, they were off—at a grandmotherly pace. "What do you think of David?"

"He's so dreamy." Emma sighed. "Even more so than his picture."

"Hey! I'm sitting right here." Joshua's words wafted forward from the back seat.

"No worries," Emma said. "I only have eyes for you."

"Good to know."

Emma returned her attention to Jennifer. "You two seem like a perfect fit."

"That's what everyone says." Jennifer smiled.

"What about your parents?" Emma asked.

"My mom adores him, and my dad says that while no one will ever be good enough for me, David is the closest anyone will ever get. And his parents think the world of me. They treat me like the daughter they've never had."

"So your family is behind you," Emma said. "That's great!"

"Yes, but I want to know what you think. Do we have your blessing to get married?"

Confused, Emma studied her teacher's face. "Are you asking for my approval?"

"I am. We are."

Emma looked out the side window. She scrunched her eyes, trying to make sense of

Jennifer's unexpected question. Though she and Joshua were in a good place, she barely had their relationship figured out. Who was she to judge someone else's?

Jennifer interrupted Emma's deliberations. "You have profound spiritual insight into people. Your opinion matters to me—to us—a lot."

Emma made a silent request for wisdom from the Sovereign before she spoke. "You two are moving in the same direction spiritually. That's critical." She paused as she considered if she should say more. "It's just that . . ."

"What?" Jennifer said. "It's just that, what?"

Emma wished she'd kept those last three words to herself, but now that she had opened the door, she had to walk through. "It's just that you have the Sovereign's Divine Spirit at work in your life, and David doesn't. This isn't a problem really, just that you have spiritual insight he lacks. That means you'll have to be the spiritual leader in your marriage."

"I never thought of that." Jennifer sighed. "I want him to be the spiritual leader. If he has the Divine Spirit in him, will that fix everything? Will you impart it into him?"

"Why don't you do it?" Emma peered at Jennifer.

"Because I can't," Jennifer said. "I don't know what to do."

"That's exactly what Chloe said when I told her to impart the Divine Spirit into you, but she did."

"It won't work for me."

"How do you know if you haven't tried?" Emma asked. "Move forward in faith and trust the Sovereign for the rest."

Jennifer remained quiet for a long time. At last she spoke. "Okay then. I'll do it the next time I see him." She inhaled slowly. "David was going to ask this, but since he's not here, will you perform the ceremony?"

Emma had a ready answer. "I would want it to align with what we read in the Holy Text."

"I'm intrigued," Jennifer said. "What would it be like?"

"Based on the examples in Scripture, it's a simple ceremony," Emma said. "As the bride, you and your parents stand to my far left. David and his parents stand to my far right. After you both pledge to a lifelong union, with your parents' support and approval, you walk toward each other, meeting me in the middle. There's a knot-tying ceremony to show you're bonded to each other. That's it. You're married. Then there's a party to celebrate."

"I like it!" Jennifer said. "It's simple and will eliminate a lot of the stress most brides face."

"Just let me know when you want to schedule it," Emma said. "I recommend a Saturday."

"David and I will discuss," Jennifer said. "But first I need to impart the Sovereign's Divine Spirit into him. Then we can move forward."

"Let me know as soon as you can," Emma said, "because another wedding is in the works."

"Who?" asked Jennifer and Joshua at the same time.

"Can't say." Emma grinned. "It's top secret."

Jennifer pulled the car into the main entrance of the Temple grounds and slowly drove back to the parking lot.

"I guess if I want to really experience riding in a sports car," Joshua said, "I'll need to have David take me for a spin."

"You are so correct," Jennifer said. "The last thing I want to do is crack up his car. But I can assure you, this car can really move—just not when I'm driving it."

Emma and Joshua climbed out of the vehicle,

thanking Jennifer for their double date, a delicious meal, and a wonderful time.

As Jennifer drove away, Chloe walked up. Emma gasped. That's when she remembered Joshua's mom always gave Chloe a ride home. Their double date had left Emma's best friend stranded.

10: ANOTHER QUESTION

Emitting a sorrowful groan, Emma ran up to Chloe with outstretched arms to hug her friend. Emma sputtered an apology. "I completely forgot that you and Joshua always ride together. So sorry I stranded you here."

"I wasn't stranded," Chloe said. "It worked out great. As soon as Joshua told me about the change in schedule, I knew that would give me more time to spend with Grandpa. We had a great time together and made an important decision."

"I'm glad it all worked out," Emma said. "It seems I'm always overlooking something—either with my friends or my job."

Joshua caught up to Emma and laid a comforting hand on her back. "You have a lot to keep straight and do a great job at it. An occasional slipup is no big deal. I let Chloe know right away. It's all good."

"Thanks," Emma said. "I so love you both."

"I texted Mom when we left the diner," Joshua said. "She should be here in about ten minutes."

Emma turned to Chloe. "What was your important decision? Is it something you can share?"

"It is," Chloe said. "And we need your help. But first, we took Montgomery for a walk. We got him settled for the night. I hope that's okay."

"That was so thoughtful of you. Did he pee? Did he poop?"

Chloe smirked. "Like I said, we got him settled for the night."

"Should I leave so you two can talk?" Joshua asked.

Chloe shook her head. "Grandpa and I decided we shouldn't hide our connection from Dad any longer. We need to come clean. And soon."

"Great idea," Emma said. "The longer you wait, the madder he's going to be."

"Oh, he's going to be mad regardless of when he finds out," Chloe said. "Grandpa thinks it should come from him, but Dad has blocked his number and email address. If he approaches Dad in person, he could have Grandpa arrested for violating the restraining order."

"What are you going to do?" Emma asked.

"It's up to me," Chloe said. "I need to do it. But if you're open to it, I'd like you to be with me. You won't need to say anything. My dad respects you and will be less likely to blow up if you're there."

"Of course, I'll help," Emma said. "That's what friends do."

"You don't need to say anything," Chloe reiterated. "Just be there and give me some moral support."

"When?" Emma asked.

"If it works for you," Chloe said, "how about tomorrow evening? Here? I could invite Dad to have supper with us in the cafeteria. Then I'll tell him."

"Do you want me to be there too?" Joshua asked.

"Thanks for the offer," Chloe said, "but he doesn't know you and might think we're ganging up on him. So you're off the hook."

"Good!" Joshua exclaimed. "But let me know if you change your mind."

"How are you going to get your dad here?" Emma asked Chloe.

"He hasn't seen you since you became High Priestess, so that's one idea," Chloe said. "He also has questions about our microschool. He's concerned I'm not getting a good education. And I haven't told him I want to become a priest. So there are a lot of reasons."

Emma wanted to talk through Chloe's partial plan, but Joshua's mother arrived, ending their conversation.

"See you tomorrow," Chloe said as she ran to the car.

11: AN EVENTFUL MORNING

Full of anticipation for the busy day in front of her, Emma and Montgomery left the cafeteria early and headed to meet Ashley at her salon before school. As soon as they entered, Montgomery strained to get away from Emma.

"Drop his leash," Ashley suggested. "I'm curious what he'll do." Her eyes sparkled.

Emma released it, and Montgomery darted to the corner of the salon where his bed had been. Even though it was no longer there, he lay down as if it were.

Ashley bounced on her toes and tapped her fingers against each other. "That's exactly what I expected. He's comfortable here. He views this as a safe place."

"That doesn't surprise me," Emma said. "What did you want to talk about?"

"I did some detective work and found out where Montgomery has been going to puppy school. It's on Saturday. I'll pick you up at two. Afterward, we can stock up on dog food and any other supplies you need."

"Thanks, but I can't pay for any of it." Emma hung her head. "I applied for a credit card so I could buy his food online, but they denied me. The automated response said I needed a better work history and to be older. I've got money in the bank, but I'm not sure how to get it out."

"No problem. I'll cover everything, and you can pay me back later—once you get things figured out."

Thanking Ashley, Emma and Montgomery hustled to school, arriving only seconds early. She unclipped his leash, and he dashed to his spot in the back. Someone—Chloe, she guessed—had already set out a water bowl for him.

Emma sat as Jennifer began. "Now that all of you working toward getting your driver's license have completed the online class, the next step is practice. On Saturday, Topher and Christopher will be here to help you with that. They'll hold a two-hour in-person class at eight. Then, starting at ten you'll take turns driving around our parking lots. Here's a sign-up sheet for you to pick your preferred time."

Jennifer handed the sheet to Emma. She scanned the options. There were four two-hour slots, with three openings per slot. Emma needed to keep her afternoon open for puppy school, so she put her name down for 10:00, a bit embarrassed about grabbing the best time. If not for her prior commitment, she'd have let everyone else pick first and she would have gone last.

Joshua and Chloe also picked 10:00, which meant they would drive together. The thought of at last getting behind the wheel of a car excited Emma. It also terrified her.

As the sign-up sheet worked its way around the room, Emma slid a note to Chloe. "When we're done with school, let's talk about tonight."

Chloe jotted something and slid it back: "Great idea!"

As was usually the case, Emma finished her schoolwork before everyone else. She quietly turned in her assignments and tiptoed to the back of the room. She clipped Montgomery's leash on his harness and slipped out to wait for Chloe in the hall.

A surprise awaited her.

It was Fred. Instead of his usual easygoing manner, he showed a stoic sternness. "We need to talk." Without another word, he turned to his left and strode toward the door. Emma followed, her pulse thumping.

Once outside, she at last caught up with him. "What's up?" Though worried about his answer, she tried to sound unconcerned.

"We'll explain everything momentarily."

His use of the pronoun *we* freaked Emma out. Her heart pounded. *Who did* we *include? Will they gang up on me? What have I done wrong? Was it an intervention?*

Fred took Emma to the palace and led her to the conference room. Christopher and Mark were waiting. They didn't look too pleased either. A meeting with the Temple's executive administrator, director of human resources, and Chief of Priests seemed as bad as it could get.

Emma sat across from Christopher and Mark. Fred walked around the table and sat between them. "We have some concerns about your latest interview with Scarlett Steele."

Emma scrunched her eyebrows. "I didn't see it, but I thought our interview went really well."

"We feel otherwise," Mark said.

"Your careless words have caused us a lot of needless work," Christopher added.

"You shouldn't have given them access to your quarters," Fred stated. "It makes it look like you're living in squalor, even though it was your choice. Viewers seem to agree and have been criticizing us online for letting it happen. They're also donating money for the upgrades—a lot."

"But I said our plans were to spruce things up a bit, and we had that covered."

"You did indeed say that," Fred said. "But you forgot to include the priests' quarters in your project summary at the end. Donations began flooding in as soon as that segment aired and continued until we shut down the online payment portal."

"But aren't donations a good thing?" Emma asked.

"Normally they are," Fred said. "But currently we don't need them. One day we will. Then we'll ask for money. But not until then. When we get to that point, we don't want people to be weary of donating."

Fred's rebuke pained Emma, but he was right.

They all were. She'd spoken without thinking. "I'm sorry for not being more careful with my words. It won't happen again."

Emma stood, but Fred motioned for her to sit. She did.

"The second problem is your premature announcement about the school to train future priests," Mark said.

"This completely blindsided our communication staff," Christopher added. "It left them scurrying to figure out how to respond to the flood of calls, emails, and texts that came in. There are a lot of angry people out there. They want to apply but can't figure out how."

Emma fought to maintain her composure. She groaned a silent prayer for strength. She closed her eyes and slowly breathed in. "I'm sorry for that too."

"Lane scrambled to add an *application* page to our website," Christopher said. "For now, it states that we're not presently taking applications for our priest school, and we'll make a formal announcement when the time comes."

"Did that solve the problem?" Emma hoped they'd say yes but feared they wouldn't.

"There's been a lot of criticism about our poor

handling of the situation," Mark said. "Once again, your zeal has preempted us from properly promoting an opportunity."

"We agree with and support your vision for training future priests," Fred said, "but we need to come to a complete understanding and have a unified front before making any public-facing announcements."

Emma could barely hold back her tears. "I understand. From now on, I won't talk about plans until they're final."

"Even more damaging was your vague reference for repurposing the space next to the cafeteria," Fred added. "The online rumor mill is rife with speculation. Conspiracy theories abound over what you intend to do with that building. It's hard to imagine a worse outcome."

Emma clamped her mouth shut and breathed through her nose. She pressed her thumbnail hard into her finger. It hurt. She hoped the pain would distract her from letting her emotions spill forth. As High Priestess, Emma had to remain strong.

"I'm sorry for that too," Emma said. "What do I need to do to fix it? To make things right?"

"First," Fred said, "let us know what your vision is—assuming you have one."

"Oh, I do. It's not a half-baked scheme. It's fully baked—mostly. I just haven't told you about it."

Emma studied the three men. They now seemed more curious than mad. "Though we have an excellent cafeteria, a food court would be a better option. It would position us for the future and serve more people. So I hope we can turn the space next to the cafeteria into a food court. We can open it to the public for moderately priced meals. They could eat there before or after the Sunday services. It would also be available for the people who come here to see the ancient Temple during the week, as well as students here for evening classes."

"What would you do with the old cafeteria?" Fred asked.

Emma sighed. "I don't have that part fully worked out yet, but I was thinking of repurposing it for overflow seating for dining and making it into a common area for people to meet and relax. We could even connect the two buildings for more space and better flow."

The three men looked at each other, but Emma had no idea what they were thinking. At last, they turned toward her. Christopher spoke. "It's an excellent vision, and I applaud your foresight. It's forward-thinking and progressive. Yet we have much to do first before we can entertain such a task."

His kind words encouraged Emma. For the first time in their meeting, they weren't confronting her mistakes. She relaxed her thumb and rubbed her finger, which was now quite sore.

"You asked how we could fix this," Fred said. "Here's what I recommend. First, we need to move you out of your quarters and into one of the newly open rooms on the first floor. With the arrest of the seven fanatic priests, their rooms are all available. I insist you move into one of them. You'll need to vacate your room when the renovation starts anyway, so why not do it now?"

"What if I don't want to?" Emma asked.

"You don't have a choice," Fred answered. "Once you've moved, let's arrange for Scarlett to see your new quarters and broadcast an update. As far as the food court debacle, I'll draft a carefully worded press release about our general intentions, clearly stating that it's a future-focused initiative that we won't even start until all our other projects are complete. Then I'll get with Scarlett to see if she can help get the word out."

"I apologize for all the problems I caused. Is there anything else we need to discuss?"

Fred nodded.

12: A BIG DEAL

Emma groaned. She wasn't sure how much more she could take without losing what little self-control she clung to. "What else?" she snapped, immediately regretting her harsh tone.

"We'll discuss it on our way to lunch," the priest said. "It's already past noon."

Emma stood and marched out of the conference room. She left the palace in a huff and headed to the cafeteria, leaving the three men behind. She tried to push the frustration from her being and asked the Sovereign for help.

Place your focus on me and remove it from yourself, came the Sovereign's wise response. *And remember to breathe.*

The Sovereign was right. Emma had been focusing on her personal embarrassment and missed the damage she caused to the Sovereign. The High Priestess repented. *I'm sorry.*

Emma slowed her harried pace to let the men catch up. Soon their footfalls reached her ears.

Fred huffed up beside her. "Imagine our surprise when the Prime Minister's advanced security detail showed up here this morning. We didn't know what was going on until Hernandez informed us you have a meeting this afternoon with the Prime Minister. You should've kept us informed."

"I didn't think it was a big deal," Emma said.

"I can assure you it's a very big deal," Fred responded. "What's on the agenda?"

"I have no idea."

"That's even worse." Fred let out a slow sigh.

Emma retrieved her phone and brought up the text message. She handed the device to Fred. He read it aloud so that Mark and Christopher—who now trailed them—could hear. "It's time for us to meet. Since you can't drive, I'll come to you. This Thursday at 3:00. -PM."

"This is bad. Really bad," Fred said. "As soon as we finish lunch, I'll spend every available minute prepping you for the meeting. We need to anticipate every possible scenario. I'll also serve as your advisor throughout and won't leave your side."

Emma turned to look at the former software VP, turned priest, turned executive administrator. "No disrespect, but what do you know about politics?"

"Quite a bit, actually. You may recall that I told you besides my MBA, my undergrad work was in poli-sci."

"I have no idea what that is."

"It stands for political science."

"Oh . . . you mean like politics?"

"Precisely."

Emma dipped her head and closed her eyes as she inhaled slowly. "Got it."

"One more thing," Fred said "Taking Montgomery to a meeting with the Prime Minister is completely inappropriate. Will it be okay for you to leave him in your room?"

Given their contentious morning, Emma knew better than to argue with Fred about it. "I have a better idea. I'll see if he can stay with Auntie Ashley."

After dropping off Montgomery with the more-than-willing cosmetologist, Fred and Emma grabbed their lunch to go. They retreated to her palace office. Soon Emma's mind was spinning with scenarios that Fred kept dumping on her. After two and a half hours of speculation, Emma was no closer to being ready for the meeting than she was before they started. In fact, she felt worse off.

Her body trembled, and her gut roiled. The one thing they hadn't done was pray. But praying and focusing her thoughts on the Sovereign's perspective was the best thing she could've done.

Yet Fred's frantic preparations distracted her from what was more important.

"I think we should pray," Emma said at last.

Fred gave her a surprised look. "You're so right."

The priest sucked in a slow breath, but Emma reacted first. "Lord, guide me in the meeting with the Prime Minister. Reveal to me what to say or not say. May all that we do and say honor you. So be it."

Hernandez and one of his security guards waited for them outside Emma's office. There was a flurry of activity, with official-looking security personnel in black suits buzzing about, preparing for the Prime Minister's arrival.

Their leader approached Hernandez. "We swept the building. It's secure and now off-limits to everyone except essential personnel." The man turned to Fred. "You must leave."

"He's my advisor," Emma said. "He is essential for the meeting."

"Very well," the security team leader said with a sigh, "but no one else. Understood?"

As Hernandez and his guard stood at the two doors to the conference room, Emma and Fred entered and sat. They waited. And they waited.

"This is a standard negotiating tactic," Fred whispered to Emma. "They arrive late to make the other party irritated and unsettled."

At 3:20, Emma heard the roar of a helicopter touching down. Seconds later, the Prime Minister's team whisked her into the conference room. Two aides trailed her, with four guards who flanked them. The guards waited outside, along with Hernandez and his man. The two aides followed the Prime Minister inside. She wore a red power suit, designer heels, and more gold jewelry than Emma had ever seen on one person.

For the first time in her life, Emma felt under-dressed. She squirmed, embarrassed over her jeans, T-shirt, and ponytail.

Fred stood to face the Prime Minister. That's when Emma remembered she was supposed to stand too. She was late, and the Prime Minister scowled at her.

"I'm pleased to meet you," said the Prime Minister at last. Her broad smile struck Emma as being both forced and fake.

Emma reached out for the handshaking ritual. But she was unprepared for the Prime Minister's vise-like grip. Emma winced, trying to squeeze back as Fred had instructed, but she failed.

At last the Prime Minister relaxed her grasp and withdrew her arm. "Have a seat," she said with a graceful gesture. The Prime Minister's aides sat, but she didn't. She glared at Emma and Fred until they sat. She was the last to do so, notching another win in her political gamesmanship.

After making introductions and gushing about her busy schedule and the many important initiatives she was undertaking, the Prime Minister turned to Fred. "Please leave us so that Emma and I may have a private conversation."

Emma was prepared for this. "He may stay. He can hear whatever you have to say."

"He may not," came the Prime Minister's terse reply.

Fred stood, but the Prime Minister's aides didn't. "If I'm leaving, they must leave too."

The Prime Minister nodded, and the two aides left the conference room. Fred followed them and pulled the door shut.

The Prime Minister relaxed her stern persona and flashed a fake smile. "I had a good working relationship with His Royal Eminence and expect that will continue with you. Can I count on your support?"

"His name is Barney." Emma glared at the Prime Minister. "He made up the title of His Royal Eminence."

"I hold you accountable for prohibiting everyone from using his worthy title, which offered him the high respect he deserved."

"We show respect by using his real name."

"Nonetheless, can I count on your support to continue with our initiatives?"

Emma looked at the Prime Minister in the spiritual realm. She possessed a glossy black visage, just like Barney. She was as evil as he was, maybe even worse. "I don't know what you and Barney were working on, but I'm quite sure I want no part of it."

The Prime Minister's friendliness washed from her face like a retreating ocean wave. "You can choose to work with me or flail against me. But know this: I don't take kindly to opposition."

Emma glared at the Prime Minister. "And I don't take kindly to threats."

"Is that your final position on the matter?"

Emma nodded. "It is."

"I'm sorry to hear that. Even though you took my beloved Bernard away from me, I had planned to give you the benefit of the doubt, to give you a chance to redeem yourself. But I see you're unredeemable. You have sealed your own fate."

"I overcame Barney in both the spiritual realm and our physical reality. I will overcome you too," Emma said. "The Sovereign is on my side."

The Prime Minister scowled at Emma. "Please call him Bernard as a show of the respect he deserves." She held her glare for several seconds as she let out a slow breath. "I care nothing about the Sovereign or your antiquated religion, but know this, Emma Barlow, I will take you down." The Prime Minister stood and jabbed a rigid finger toward Emma's upturned eyes. "Though Bernard failed, I will not." She relaxed her glare, held her head high, and marched out of the conference room. Her aides fell into step behind her as her security detail surrounded her and ushered her away.

Fred rushed into the room. Seconds later they heard the helicopter lift off.

"I'm glad that's over," he said.

"It isn't over," Emma said. "It's only just begun."

13: A FATEFUL SUPPER

Emma told Fred what the Prime Minister had said and the threat she made. They speculated on what Emma might face and how to prepare.

Fred said, "I suggest I talk to Barney and see if he can give us insight into what the Prime Minister is talking about."

Emma shook her head. "When Hernandez went to the prison, Barney said that going forward he'd only talk to me, which I hope to avoid."

"You should not have to see him—ever again. Let's pray for supernatural insight."

Emma agreed, but a text message arrived before they could begin.

It was from Chloe. "Is it going to work out for you to meet with my dad at the cafeteria?"

With a moan, Emma brought her elbows to the table and lowered her head to rest on her hands. "I'm such a lousy friend. I completely forgot about meeting Chloe's dad tonight. I didn't even get together with her after school to discuss it, as I'd promised."

"That's on me," Fred said. "I'll let her know it's not your fault."

Emma ignored what Fred said. She texted Chloe. "On my way." Without a word, she left Fred. It was, after all, sort of his fault.

Emma met Chloe at the cafeteria. "So sorry. Some unexpected things came up," Emma said. "But I'm here now." She didn't mention Fred, even though she wanted to blame him.

Then another text arrived. It was from Ashley. "I fed Montgomery and took him for a walk. He's ready for the night, snuggled on your bed."

Emma wanted to scream. Not only had she forgotten her commitment to Chloe, but she had also forgotten her responsibility of having a dog to care for. "I'm such a bad puppy parent," she texted back. "Thanks for covering. You're the best."

Chloe's dad arrived seconds later. He gave

Emma a friendly hug. "It's good to see you, Emma. It's been too long." With a sly smirk, he tipped his head down. "High Priestess."

"Dad!" Chloe hissed. "Remember what I told you."

"It was just a joke." He winked at Emma.

"It's all good," Emma said to Chloe. "Let's grab some food."

Chloe led the way, her dad followed, and Emma took up the rear.

"I'd like to hear more about the homeschool situation here at the Temple," he said to Emma as they selected their food. "I have concerns."

"We moved from homeschool to a microschool," Emma said. "Jennifer Russell heads it up. She's a certified teacher. It's going really well. We're already ahead of where we should be at this point in the school year."

"I appreciate knowing this," Mr. Cruz said. "But will Chloe be adequately prepared for college when she graduates? Assuming there's even a graduation."

"I'm not planning to go to college, Dad," Chloe said. "I want to become a priest."

Mr. Cruz didn't say more until they were situated at a table in the back corner of the cafeteria. "I don't have any problem with you being High Priestess, Emma, but I don't see the priesthood as being a realistic option for my daughter's future."

Emma relaxed her tense shoulders and smiled. "The priests confirmed my understanding that there's nothing in the Holy Text to prevent women from being priests. It's more a cultural thing. Along with Chloe, five of our friends are also planning to become female priests. Chloe will break new ground."

Mr. Cruz laughed. "I think you've already done that!"

Chloe inhaled loudly, and her dad stopped eating to wait for what she was about to say. "Aside from telling you about school and that I want to become a priest, I also want to talk about Grandpa."

Mr. Cruz slammed his fork on the table. "I don't!"

"He's a really nice man," Chloe said. "He reminds me a lot of you."

"You mean you've met him?" Mr. Cruz raised his voice. "He's under a restraining order. I'll have him arrested! Do you know where he is?"

"I suppose somewhere here on the Temple grounds," Chloe said. "He lives here."

"You mean I granted my daughter permission to go to school so she could be near the man I strictly forbade her to be around?" He pounded his fist on the table. "Emma, did you know about this?"

"He's my mentor. I suggested Chloe meet with him, too, but he avoided her for the longest time. Once they met, she quickly figured it out. That's the first I knew that he's your father."

Mr. Cruz set his jaw and pounded both fists on the table. Their trays rattled at the impact.

Emma continued. "I don't know what Gabe did, but he's a new man. He's gentle and kind and wise. His prayer is that one day you'll be able to see how much he's changed, in hopes he can again be part of your life and Chloe's."

Mr. Cruz stood so fast that his chair fell backward, clattering on the floor. He glared down at Emma, jabbing a finger at her face. "High Priestess or not, I hold you completely responsible for what's happened." Then he stomped out of the cafeteria as everyone watched him in wide-eyed shock.

Panting, one of Hernandez's security guards rushed up. "High Priestess, are you okay?"

"No worries," Emma said. "It was just a little misunderstanding."

"I'm relieved," he said. "I'll track him down and escort him from the premises."

Emma held up her hand. "No need. He just needs time to cool off."

"Nevertheless, I will stay nearby to protect you if needed, along with everyone else here." The guard stepped back, planted his feet, and crossed his arms.

Worry covered Chloe's face. "What are we going to do now?"

"We're going to pray." Emma grasped Chloe's hand. "Sovereign Lord, be with Mr. Cruz as he processes this news, and help him calm down. May Chloe's dad not have Gabe arrested. Also, keep them away from each other until Mr. Cruz can be civil."

"And please keep Grandpa safe," Chloe added.

"Amen," Emma concluded.

The girls opened their eyes and looked at each other, full of concern, but Emma remained expectant for the Sovereign's answer to their prayers.

"Should we go look for them?" Chloe asked.

"I think we should stay here and wait," Emma answered. "Let your dad come to us."

Then Emma texted Gabe. "Things didn't go well, and he's mad! We're praying."

Chloe fidgeted and blinked rapidly. "I'm so worried about Dad—and Grandpa."

"We prayed for them both and now we must trust the Sovereign with the rest," Emma said. She studied her best friend's face and decided to distract Chloe. "Last evening Joshua told me he wants to help with the traditional service. That really surprised me."

"I knew it would," Chloe said. "It surprised us all. But it makes sense."

"I didn't realize you were discussing potential roles."

"We've all been sharing our ideas," Chloe said. "About half of us have decided and the rest are close."

"What do you want to do?" Emma asked.

"William wants to work at the ancient Temple, Lane is interested in tech, and Kayla wants to head up the communications department."

"Beatrice handles communications."

"But she doesn't want to," Chloe countered. "She's thinking of resigning. They hired her as a receptionist, and that's what she wants to do—not managing people or handling email and stuff. She enjoys talking on the phone. None of the rest of us do."

"Will Beatrice wait until Kayla can take over? That will be a couple of years at least."

"We wondered if a priest could help Kayla right away to take some of the pressure off Beatrice."

"That's it!" Emma exclaimed. "That's the missing piece. Though I have a mentor, none of you do. I think everyone needs a mentor to help them move into their area of focus. That's brilliant!"

"Don't thank me. It was your idea."

"What about you?" Emma asked. "What do you want to do?"

"I want to form a new position to handle online communications. Lane said he could teach me how to add pages to the website, and I could keep everything up to date. But the site also needs a complete makeover. With Lane's help on the technical stuff, I'll do that. We need a social media presence too. I also want to make a website for you, as High Priestess."

Emma shook her head. "I don't want to call attention to myself. My goal is to point people to the Sovereign."

"I agree. That's what I want your website to do. We can't know what the Sovereign looks like, but we all know what you look like. You are our faith's visual representation."

"I'm still uncomfortable with it," Emma said.

"Did you know that about one fourth of our text messages and over one third of our email messages relate to you? Having a website and social media accounts for you would handle most of it."

"I already have social media accounts."

"Those are personal accounts," Chloe said. "As High Priestess, you need professional accounts too. I'll do them for you, and you won't need to do a thing. And we could post your insights about the Holy Text on your website and link to them from social. That would definitely point people to the Sovereign."

Emma smiled as she thought about all the possible content. "I'll consider it. Will you work up a plan?"

"Already on it!"

Emma touched Chloe's hand. "You're wonderful. I don't deserve a friend as good as you."

"I was thinking the same thing about you. Except for Dad being angry at Grandpa, all the good things happening in my life right now are because of you."

Emma looked about in confusion. The normal

chatter in the cafeteria had lessened. Soon it became completely quiet. Emma scanned the room to see why. Everyone was staring at the main entrance. Mr. Cruz stood there. Once he had everyone's attention, he extended his right arm.

"I apologize for my earlier outburst. My anger got the best of me, and I was out of line. I was wrong to blame the High Priestess for my frustration. She did nothing wrong. Though you don't know me, you may know my daughter, Chloe." He pointed to her.

"You may also know my father, Gabriel. I blamed him for something that was as much my fault as his. I pushed him out of my life and shouldn't have. But I'm pleased to say he has accepted my apology." Mr. Cruz stretched out his left arm, and Gabe walked up next to him.

"Thank you, Lord," Chloe whispered.

Everyone in the cafeteria cheered.

With tears flowing, Chloe sprang from the table and ran toward them with outstretched arms.

14: TGIF

Overflowing with joy for Chloe's dad and Gabe reconnecting, Emma finished her nightly study of the Holy Text, turned out the lights, and slid into bed. Montgomery bounded up next to her. He snuggled down, and she stroked his back as she reviewed her day and thanked the Sovereign for helping her through it. She soon fell asleep.

The next morning at breakfast, the only thing the priests wanted to talk about was Gabe being reunited with his estranged son. Gabe had endeared himself to every one of them, and they celebrated his exciting news.

Emma blessed them and dashed off to school.

Joshua met her just outside the cafeteria. "I hear you had quite a day yesterday. How are you doing?"

"Thank goodness it's Friday," Emma said. "Yesterday is a day I hope to never repeat, but it ended well. Did you hear about Chloe's dad and grandpa?"

Joshua nodded. "I know this is last minute. I wanted to ask yesterday but never got the chance. Would you like to have dinner tonight at my house and meet my parents? I've met yours, but you haven't met mine. If tonight won't work out, maybe sometime next week? Another option would be to—"

Emma brought her finger gently to his lips to stop him from rambling. "Tonight would be perfect."

They headed toward school, with Joshua on her left and Montgomery heeling on her right. The trio rounded a curve in the path and spotted Ashley walking toward them.

"Montgomery had such a great time in my shop yesterday. Might he like to hang out there today too?"

"Does it make me a bad puppy parent if I say yes?"

"Not at all," Ashley said. "Just think of me as

doggy daycare. During the workday he can help me welcome clients. He'll spend the evenings and weekends with you."

Emma handed Ashley Montgomery's leash. "Today can be a test. If everything works out, we can consider doing it every day. Should I get his doggie bed from my room?"

"It's not there," Ashley said with a grin. "Since he sleeps with you, I grabbed his bed last night."

Emma smiled. "You two have a great day." As Ashley and Montgomery walked away, Emma sniffed. "I know it's a good idea, but I feel kind of sad."

Joshua put his arm around Emma's shoulder. "That just gives us more undistracted time."

They were almost to the school building when a grinning Chloe ran up. "Thanks for all you did last night. We're so grateful."

Emma smiled but shook her head. "All I did was pray. The Sovereign did the rest."

"Grandpa said after he got your text about Dad blowing up, he asked the Sovereign what to do. The answer came right away. It was to go to the bench by the pond and wait. Dad happened by soon after that. There was some yelling at first and then hugs and finally tears."

"So they're all good?" Emma asked.

"More than good," Chloe said. "Dad invited Grandpa to come home with us last night. They're getting along just great. He's going to move in tonight. The only bad part is, since our house has just two bedrooms, Grandpa had to sleep on the couch. It's just a thought—and feel free to say no. Seriously, I mean it. But I heard you're moving to a bigger room. What would you think about me rooming with you during the week?"

"If Gabe is moving out," Joshua said, "that means his room in the priests' quarters is available. As the best and biggest, why don't you move there?"

Before Emma could say no, Joshua continued. "The priests are honored that you want to live in the priests' quarters, but none of them like that you picked the worst room for yourself. With Gabe's room available, I think they'll insist you take it."

Emma smiled. "It doesn't sound like I have a choice, does it? Besides, I'll need the extra space for my new roomie."

15: THE ARCHITECT

After school, Emma strolled to the cafeteria for lunch. Their architect, Aurora Blake, was there to share her initial plans for the Temple welcome center with the leadership team.

Emma and Aurora chatted as they waited for everyone to arrive. "Architecture is kind of my hobby," Emma said. "Before I came here, I was studying to be an architect."

"Even as a young girl, I wanted to be one," Aurora said. "Design is my passion. I relish creating compelling visions for new construction. But just as much, I delight in reworking existing buildings to elevate them to greater functionality. A lot of architects avoid renovation projects, but they're my specialty."

"We're planning a lot of renovation here on the Temple grounds," Emma said.

"I know. I hope I'll have a chance to bid on that work. But first things first."

Emma glanced at the plans rolled up in Aurora's hand. "I can't wait to see your design for the welcome center."

"And I can't wait to show you." Aurora unfurled her plans on the table.

Emma edged up to study them. "It's a brilliant design. I like the flow of your interior layout and especially appreciate how well the exterior aligns with the ancient Temple. It's obviously modern but doesn't at all look out of place. You're very talented."

"You're most kind," Aurora said.

Emma gobbled her lunch as she paged through the preliminary drawings. Aurora had already eaten and explained her design choices to Emma.

Once everyone arrived, Aurora went through the plans again. Everyone thought they were great, and no one had any suggestions or changes. "The price even came in under budget."

Ezra was especially excited. "How soon can we move forward?"

"As soon as I have your approval," Aurora said. "What makes me unique among architects is that I can also serve as the construction manager, so if you'd like, I can handle that aspect as well. Most of my clients appreciate me being a full-service provider, moving a project from concept to completion."

"Sounds good to me," Emma said. She glanced at Fred, allowing him to get the team's consensus and confirm their decision. He did, granting Aurora the authority to move forward.

"All my contacts in the trades are clamoring to be involved with this project," Aurora said. "We should be able to break ground on Monday and complete it within six weeks."

As Aurora rolled up her plans, Fred had an update to share. "The bid to replace the lead pipe in the High Priest's residence in the palace is astronomical. It will take months and be disruptive. I'll get more bids, but I'm not optimistic."

"Why so much?" Emma asked. "I thought only about twelve feet of pipe needs to be replaced."

"Correct," Fred responded, "but the pipe is

encased in concrete, which is an integral structural element. Hence the reason for the high cost."

Emma cocked her head and looked at Fred. "Did you ask them for a quote to replace the piping?"

Fred nodded.

"Why don't you bring in a different plumber and ask for a quote to cap the bad piping and reroute the line around it?"

"That is a most astute recommendation, High Priestess," Aurora said. "I was about to suggest that myself."

"My dad uses Paul's Plumbing and says he's the best," Emma said. "He's honest, fair, and does quality work."

"I can vouch for him," Aurora said. "I've used him on some of my projects. If you want, I'll text him for a quote." She pulled out her phone.

With lunch over, Emma's team dispersed, but she signaled for Fred to stay. "How are you doing with plans to fix the dorm rooms and redo the priests' quarters?"

Fred sighed. "Not well. The firms I contacted seem to only take on renovation projects if they need the work, and everyone I talk to is plenty busy."

Aurora perked up, her gaze darting between Emma and Fred, but she pursed her lips. She put her phone back in her bag and smiled. "Paul is on his way here for your plumbing issue."

Fred looked at Aurora and raised his eyebrows. "That was fast."

"The trades like working with me and are always responsive," Aurora said. "When I need help, they make me a priority."

That's when Emma made her pitch to Fred. "Not only does Aurora design new buildings, but she specializes in renovations. Can we show her what we need?"

"I have the afternoon open," Aurora said.

"I'll text Gabe to see if he can cover for me in discussing the Holy Text with the priests," Emma said. "Though I don't want to reschedule my meeting with Jennifer later this afternoon, I'm available for the next three hours."

Fred smiled. "As you would say, Emma, let's do this!"

"Where should we start?" Aurora asked.

Fred shrugged. "Since these are Emma's ideas, I suggest she take the lead. My goal is simply to facilitate what she envisions."

"Since it's the closest, let's start with the priests'

quarters—even though it's the lowest priority," Emma announced. "That will also let me grab my sketches."

Emma led Aurora and Fred to the priests' quarters, which was right next to the cafeteria. She opened the door to her room and invited Aurora in. Fred waited outside. "Though my room is smaller than the rest of them, it gives you an idea of what the other rooms on this floor look like. This is the level we need renovated. The upper two floors are fine."

Aurora glanced around the dated room. It only took her a few seconds. "I agree with your concerns."

"Here's a rough sketch of the current floor plan." Emma showed her drawing to Aurora. "The lighting here isn't good. Let's step outside so we can see better."

Aurora studied Emma's sketch. "This is most helpful."

"There are eighteen rooms on this level," Emma said. "Seventeen are occupied."

"Your lines reveal an engaging style," Aurora said. "I'm impressed."

"And here are my ideas for the changes." Emma moved the first sketch to the bottom of the pile to reveal a second drawing. "There will be ten rooms, five on each side. That will make them about the same size as the rooms on the second level, but smaller than the rooms on the third floor."

Fred edged up and looked over Emma's shoulder. "I must point out that the numbers don't work. This design—while impressive—eliminates eight rooms. Where will the other priests live? Another concern is where they'll stay during the renovations, which will displace seventeen people—you and sixteen priests."

"With the arrest of the seven fanatic priests, we now have seven open rooms on the upper level," Emma said. "Those rooms are much larger, and we can easily put two priests in each room. They'll even have more space! And we can overflow into the palace if we need to. There are a lot of unused bedrooms and baths there."

"What about for the long term?"

Emma smiled, her eyes twinkling. "The Sovereign told me that won't be an issue."

"Can you explain?" Fred asked.

"I hope it's because of my plan to send some priests to work in other districts."

"Your sketches provide helpful information," Aurora said. "The major problem is re-running the water and sewer lines. It will require cutting into the concrete slab, which will be expensive and time-consuming—not to mention noisy."

"The good news is it isn't a slab subfloor," Emma said. "There's a crawlspace, which gives access."

Fred shook his head. "It seems you have this all figured out."

"And she saved me several hours of work," Aurora said.

"The dorm rooms are a higher priority," Emma said. "Let's check them out. I have sketches for them too."

"I have no doubt." Fred shook his head. "You continue to amaze me."

As they walked toward the dorm rooms, Emma gave Aurora an overview. "The present configuration has small dorm rooms with only enough space for two beds and desks. Each floor has one shared bathroom and shower area. What I see is suites, with each suite having two two-person rooms and a common bathroom in between."

"That design has merit," Aurora said, "but a more contemporary configuration would be one-person rooms with private toilets and showers."

"I considered that," Emma explained, "but I

don't plan on students being in their rooms other than to sleep. Learning to share is part of their training. Besides, if they think they deserve their own room to go to school, I don't want them here."

Fred turned to Aurora. "Do you have what you need to get started?"

"Emma provided me with the essentials, but it would be helpful for me to see the big picture. I understand that it's future focused, but what are your plans relating to the cafeteria?"

"I'd like to convert the space next to the cafeteria into a food court," Emma said. "Then we'll renovate the cafeteria for overflow seating and a common area for people to hang out. I'd also like to connect the two buildings."

"That's helpful background," Aurora said. "One last question. It relates to finances. Will you be conducting a fundraising campaign or take out loans?"

"We're in a most fortunate financial situation," Fred said. "Several unexpected events have occurred, and I believe we have enough money on hand to cover all four projects. Topher researched typical renovation costs per square foot relevant to the type and scope of each project. Based on that, we can cover everything. We'll even have a twenty percent contingency fund, but I hope we won't have to touch it and can reserve it for the future."

Aurora glanced at Emma and then returned her gaze to Fred. She brought her finger to her lips. "Are you open to a bold proposal?"

Emma couldn't contain herself. "Yes!"

16: THE PLANS

Emma looked at Aurora with wide-eyed excitement. Fred scowled at the High Priestess but then softened when he turned his gaze to Aurora.

"I propose you let me be the architect and construction manager for all four projects." Aurora held her gaze steady. "I'll start with the welcome center, and next the priests' quarters and dorms, and the food court and cafeteria last. I'll commit 100 percent of my time to the projects and move strategically from one to the other, maximizing efficiency and speeding toward completion."

"Will you do the dorms first and then the priests' quarters?" Emma asked.

"We certainly can, but the priests' quarters is a

simpler project, while the dorm rooms are more involved. It will be more efficient and quicker overall to do the priests' quarters before the dorms."

"That certainly sounds reasonable," Fred said. "Please put together a formal proposal for us to consider."

"I'll have it for you first thing Monday," Aurora said. "But for right now, I need to finalize the plans for the welcome center and begin scheduling the trades."

Emma cocked her head to the side, wondering if she should say anything. Fred might object, but she felt she should ask anyway. "Will it help you if we provide office space for you here on the Temple grounds?"

"That would definitely be beneficial," Aurora said. "Thanks for asking."

Fred stroked his beard. "Neither Mark nor Christopher needs to have an office in the palace. It's not an ideal location for either, and they're rarely there. I suspect they would gladly move someplace else to give you an office."

"What else can we do to help you make this happen?" Emma asked.

Aurora inhaled slowly. "Not to be presumptuous, but you mentioned having extra sleeping quarters in the palace. If it makes sense for you to allocate one to me, that will help even more. Then I can be on site 24/7. But if you're not open to it, forget that I brought it up."

Fred nodded. "Assuming we accept your proposal, we can certainly make that happen."

"Unless there's anything else you want to cover, I'll leave and get started right away," Aurora said. She extended her hand to shake Fred's. "I hope we'll be able to work together. This is an exciting project for me both professionally and personally."

Aurora turned to Emma and extended her hand to the High Priestess. But Emma didn't want to shake hands. Bouncing on her toes, she opened her arms wide and enveloped Aurora. "I sense we'll be working together on this. You're the answer to my prayers!"

"I have a good feeling about this too," Aurora whispered. She took a step back from Emma, waved goodbye to Fred, and left.

"Aurora's involvement does seem to be the Sovereign's provision," Fred said to Emma as the architect walked away. "But let's not get ahead of ourselves. We need to see her proposal first."

"I understand," Emma said, "but I foresee that we'll accept it."

Before Fred could respond, Emma's phone chirped a reminder. "I'm off to meet with Jennifer and finalize our plans to reopen the school for the priests."

Fred held up the palm of his hand toward Emma. "I proclaim the Sovereign's blessings on you as you meet. May your plans honor our Lord."

Grateful for his thoughtfulness, Emma hustled off to her office and hoped to make it there before Jennifer. With one plan nearly in place, she had one more to complete.

Emma did indeed get there first and asked for the Sovereign's blessing on their meeting and inspiration from the Divine Spirit. Jennifer arrived just as Emma had refocused her attention.

"There's something missing from our plan, but I think we're close to finished," Jennifer said. "I pray we'll be able to put the final touches on it today and move forward."

"I think I know what's missing," Emma said. "Though I have a mentor, none of my disciples do. I think each one of them needs a priest to mentor them. That will help the students grow in their faith and move toward becoming priests. It will also let the priests help the students and feel better about the program."

"That's brilliant!" Jennifer said. "That is indeed the missing element. I agree with your recommendation and your assessment."

"That covers the Temple high school," Emma said. "For adults—if they've been to seminary—I think they must come here for at least one year to study the Holy Text and practice applying it."

"I agree," Jennifer said. "I think our priests here are all in agreement. But others who have gone to seminary and assume they're qualified will be disappointed—even angry."

Emma considered what to say. She paused as she waited for direction from the Divine Spirit. Supernatural insight soon arrived. "What if we have them fill out an application and submit an essay on why they want to be a priest here? Maybe we should give them a test about the Holy Text."

"You're thinking like a teacher." Jennifer smiled but then frowned. "Should the test be so hard that no one passes?"

Emma shook her head. "It doesn't need to be impossible, just thorough. Mostly it's to prove that seminary didn't adequately train them in the Holy Text."

"You are most astute."

Emma received Jennifer's compliment.

"Though we're moving forward with plans to reno-vate the dorms, I don't want to wait until they're done before we reopen the school. For the first year, let's limit it to people who live locally and won't need housing. What do you think?"

"That's an excellent idea. I'll add these items to our plan for both the Temple high school and adult priest training. I'll send it to you to review and then forward it to Frederick."

Though Emma really wanted to approve Jennifer's revisions, she also knew she needed to stop trying to be a part of every decision. She had a team of capable people to help her, and she needed to get out of their way and let them do their jobs.

With a gentle smile, Emma shook her head. "Not necessary. Just send us both a copy."

"Will do."

"Great!" Emma said. "Got to run. I need to first pick up Montgomery from Ashley. Then I'm meeting Joshua's parents tonight for dinner."

"That's a big step. Are you nervous?"

"It's just dinner." Emma cocked her head and peered at Jennifer. "Should I be worried?"

17: MEET THE PARENTS

Having fed and walked Montgomery, Emma ambled up to Joshua, with her puppy prancing at her side. "Where's Chloe? Your mom could be here any minute."

"Chloe's not riding with us tonight. Her dad's coming, and they'll move Gabe from his room to their house."

"So I guess it's just the two of us."

"The two of us . . . and Montgomery . . . and my sister . . . and my parents."

"Yeah . . . and your parents." Emma shifted from her right foot to her left and back again. Her gaze darted away from Joshua. She peered into the horizon and let out a slow sigh. She stared at nothing and thought of meeting Joshua's parents for the first time.

"You okay?" Joshua asked.

"Fine. No problem." Emma's eyes fluttered. She sucked in a slow breath as she attempted to corral her raging worry. "That's not true. I'm a bit nervous about meeting your parents. Terrified, actually. What if they don't like me? What if they decide they don't want us to get married?"

Joshua's shoulders shook. He threw his head back and laughed. "There's nothing to worry about. They already like you."

"So I don't need to win them over or try to impress them?"

"They're already impressed. If anything, they're worried you might not like them."

"No problem. I already do."

A car Emma didn't recognize roared up and screeched to a stop. The driver jumped out. It was Principal Johnson! *What's he doing here?*

Flushed and flustered, he blurted, "Emma, I don't want a record of what I'm about to say. In person is my only option." He cast a wary eye at Joshua. "This applies to you too. It's top secret."

Emma's worry shifted from meeting Joshua's parents to Principal Johnson's troubling arrival.

"Something's coming down," he whispered. "I fear it's bad. District officials spent most of the day in my office going through our records of students being homeschooled. Their focus seemed to be on you two and the other students here. Your teacher and her paperwork all checked out. But they question her credentials to have more than ten students. In the past it's a minor detail they always overlooked, but I think they want to turn it into an issue and shut your school down."

Emma gasped. "Can they do that?"

Principal Johnson nodded. "There's more. On Lane's paperwork, his mother didn't date her signature, and Isabella's dad initialed her paperwork but didn't sign. Usually neither is an issue, but technically it voids both documents."

"What can we do to fix it?" Emma whispered back.

"Have them drop off fully completed paperwork first thing Monday morning. It may not fully solve everything, but it will mitigate the situation."

"I'll tell them both tomorrow morning," Emma said.

Principal Johnson glanced to his right and then left. "I must go," he hissed. "I've already been here too long." He took two steps toward his car and then spun around. "I could lose my job over this, so don't tell anyone I was here or warned you."

"Promise," Emma and Joshua said at the same time.

As Principal Johnson drove away, Joshua's mom pulled her vehicle to where they stood. She jumped out and ran up to Emma, wrapping her arms around the startled High Priestess. "I'm so excited to meet you at last. I've been waiting for this day forever. So has Joshua's dad."

Joshua escorted Emma around the car and opened the front passenger-side door. With a sweep of his hand, he signaled for her to get in. When she didn't move, he laid his hand on her lower back and gave her a gentle nudge. She climbed in. He opened the back door and sat behind her.

Though Emma wanted to talk with Joshua about Principal Johnson's worrisome warning, she knew she should try to connect with his mother instead. But school was all that came to her mind. "Mrs. Hart, what do you think about Joshua going to our microschool instead of public school?"

"It's a great fit for him! We couldn't be more excited. He's learning what he needs to graduate, studying the Holy Text, and preparing to become a priest. He has meaningful work to do. I don't think I've ever seen him this happy. By the way, feel free to call me Maggie, though Mrs. Hart will do in a pinch. I'm not opposed to you calling me Mom either—not to imply I'm trying to replace yours. But I'd be honored if you'd consider me like a second mom. Just think of me as—"

"Mom," Joshua interrupted, "you're rambling."

"Sorry. I'm a little bit nervous, and you know how I ramble when I get nervous."

This made so much sense. Emma now knew where Joshua's sister, Sarah, got her proficiency at nonstop talking. Emma smiled as she considered each name Mrs. Hart had suggested. "For now, how about I call you Maggie?"

Mrs. Hart smiled. "That would be wonderful." Her eyes fluttered.

With this initial awkwardness behind them, Emma and Mrs. Hart talked for the rest of the trip.

"I made baked spaghetti tonight," Mrs. Hart said. "It's in the oven now and should be done about the time we get there."

"Spaghetti is my favorite!" Emma licked her lips.

"I know." Then Mrs. Hart explained. "Your

mom told me. I hope you don't mind me asking her."

When they walked into the house, the most mouthwatering aromas greeted them. Montgomery looked expectedly at Emma, even though he'd already eaten. A recording of pipe organ music played softly in the background. Mr. Hart poured glasses of water as Sarah set the table.

"Smells delicious," Emma said.

Sarah looked up with a start and dropped her handful of knives and forks on the table. Squealing with delight, she ran up to Emma and gave her an enormous hug. "I'm so geeked to see you again. I got questions about what we talked about. Lots of them. I met with Mr. Gabe once, but I'd rather talk to you. Can we talk after dinner? Maybe we can. I so hope so. I made a list. Let me get it."

Sarah dashed from the room, and Emma finished setting the table. As Joshua placed the water glasses on the table, Mr. Hart dished up the vegetables, while Mrs. Hart—that is, Maggie—pulled the spaghetti from the oven.

They sat at the table just as Sarah rushed back. Mr. Hart gave the opening blessing and soon they were feasting on a tasty meal.

"The spaghetti is delicious," Emma said. "But I knew it would be. You're a wonderful cook."

Joshua cocked his head to the side and narrowed his gaze at Emma. "How do you know?"

"Because she sent Sarah to the treehouse with supper and breakfast for me the night I slept there."

"What? You slept in my treehouse? When?"

"The night before I became High Priestess," Emma said. "You'd been arrested and the police were looking for me. I knew I couldn't go home, and school wasn't an option. The Sovereign had showed me a treehouse in a dream and told me it was a safe place."

"The Sovereign showed you my treehouse in a dream?" Joshua shook his head.

"I didn't know it was yours. And I didn't know whose backyard it was in. I just knew it was a safe place to spend the night."

"Mom saw Emma climb the ladder to the treehouse as we were doing dishes," Sarah added. "She said we needed to help Emma. We couldn't invite her inside because the police were waiting for her out front. But when it got dark, Mom sent me out with food and a sleeping bag."

"How did you know it was her?" Joshua asked. "You'd never seen her."

"Her picture had been on TV and social media all day long," Mr. Hart said. "By that evening, everyone knew what she looked like. Though we didn't dare risk letting her sleep in the house in case the police checked, we left the back door open for her in case she needed to use the bathroom."

"So glad you did," Emma said. "Else I don't know what I would've done."

Joshua shook his head. "I can't believe it. You slept in my treehouse, ate Mom's food, and you've been inside our home. How come no one ever told me?"

Maggie shrugged. "We were preoccupied with Emma becoming High Priestess and getting you released from jail. That's what mattered. We all forgot about the treehouse."

As they continued to enjoy the meal, they recalled what had happened on that pivotal day and all that had happened since—especially for Joshua being shot and Emma raising him from the dead.

Maggie served cannoli for dessert. When everyone finished, she gave the meal's concluding prayer, and Sarah read a section from the Holy Text.

As they stood to clear the table, Sarah looked at Emma. "May I take Montgomery for a walk?"

Emma wanted to say no, but that would make her an overprotective puppy parent. She thought better of it. "Sure!" She handed Sarah his leash and a poop bag. "To use it, just slide your hand inside and—"

"Emma, I know how to handle poop!" Sarah exclaimed. Then she froze. Everyone did. Sarah's face turned red.

When Emma laughed, everyone relaxed. "You two have fun."

After Sarah and Montgomery left, the four of them finished cleaning up from the meal and retreated to the living room to sing songs. Sarah and Montgomery returned just in time to join them. Mr. Hart played their electronic keyboard, set to sound like a pipe organ. Though Emma was skeptical about singing to organ music, she soon found herself enjoying it—a lot. She threw herself into it.

"You have a beautiful voice," Maggie said to Emma.

"That's why she has landed the lead in most every musical," Joshua added.

Emma beamed.

Joshua's parents were delightful, and they embraced her as family. She couldn't have had a better time. They sang until after 10:00, and the evening ended too soon.

Mr. Hart and Joshua took Emma and Montgomery back to the Temple grounds. Emma and Joshua both needed a good night's rest. They wanted to be at their best for their drivers' training in the morning.

18: ASH

Saturday morning, Emma and her friends sat in their regular classroom. Montgomery hunkered in his usual place in back. Christopher and Topher went through their in-person part of drivers' training. It was all review for Emma, and her mind drifted to other thoughts.

She hadn't gotten as much sleep as she wanted. She had arrived home late and felt too tired to study the Holy Text. But she had never missed a night yet and didn't want to start now. She debated what to do, but the Sovereign gave her clarity. *Just reread the two History passages that describe marriage ceremonies.*

Emma did and went to bed. The next thing she knew, it was morning. And now she sat in the classroom, waiting for her practical driving instruction to begin at 10:00. At last, it was time to drive.

Isabella, William, and Tyler got in the first car with Christopher.

Emma, Joshua, and Chloe climbed in the second car with Topher. Both Joshua and Chloe took to the driving with ease, steering around the red cones in the Temple parking lot, signaling their turns, and practicing parallel parking. Emma, however, struggled. A lot. She wanted to cry.

Chloe offered comfort. "Shake it off, bestie. Though most everything is easy for you, this is one thing you'll need to work at. Don't worry. You can do it!"

A few minutes before noon, Topher announced they were done for the day. "We'll do another session next Saturday, and then you'll be ready to get your provisional licenses."

As Joshua and Chloe climbed out of the backseat, Topher signaled for Emma to stay.

"I'll tell Lane and Isabella about resubmitting their paperwork for school," Joshua whispered to Emma. As he left, Emma saw Chloe give him a worried look.

It wasn't until they were out of earshot that Topher spoke. "I didn't want to mention it in front of your friends, but you'll need an extra hour or two of driving. We can do it some evening next week. Then you can finish up with everyone else next Saturday. How's that sound?"

"Thanks for being patient," Emma said. "For some reason, I'm having trouble making the car do what I want it to do."

"Just give yourself some grace—and relax."

As Emma considered his advice, her phone chirped. It was a text from Angie. "Gabe moved out of his quarters last night, and we cleaned it this morning. I helped moved your things to it, and you're all set."

Though Emma was irritated at Fred for making her move, she shouldn't dump her frustration on Angie, who was only doing what Fred had said. Emma breathed out slowly to release the tension building inside and typed a quick response: "Sorry you had to work on your day off. Thanks."

"No problem. I planned to be here anyway."

Christopher's car pulled into a nearby parking space, and his three students climbed out. Wide smiles covered their faces. Christopher watched them leave and then leaned against the car, like he was waiting for someone.

Emma turned back to Topher and ran her hand over the dashboard. "Nice car. Is it yours?"

Topher laughed. "It belongs to the Temple. They both do. At your suggestion, we sold the town cars and the limo and replaced them with three practical vehicles. This is one of them."

"I'd been meaning to ask Christopher about that."

"We sold both town cars for a fair price. But there was a bidding war for the limo when they learned you had ridden in it. It went for over ten times street value."

"Cool!" Emma said. "But I'm not sure what to think about it being worth more just because I rode in it."

Topher shrugged. "Embrace it." He inhaled with deliberation. "I have an important question. Ashley and I want to get married as soon as we can afford a place to live. Will you perform the ceremony?"

"Congratulations!" Emma exclaimed. "I'd be honored. What do you think about following the Holy Text for the ceremony? It's simple yet profound. I re-read those passages last night."

"Sounds good. I'm sure Ash will agree. We don't want anything fancy—or expensive. We just want to get married and can't wait. Well . . . we are waiting, but it's hard."

As Emma considered how to respond to Topher's admission, a car approached and distracted her. It was Angie. Christopher climbed in. The two leaned toward each other and shared a kiss. Then they drove away.

Topher smiled. "Dad and Angie were secretly seeing each other several years ago. But when Barney found out, he threatened to fire them both. They committed to make their service here to the Sovereign a priority and broke things off. But after you healed Dad and he returned to work, they reconnected. They want to get married too. But they're waiting for Ash and me to get married first and move out. Dad's place isn't big enough for four people."

"If a place to live is all that's stopping you, I have an idea. As soon as the lead problem in the High Priest's quarters is fixed, you could live there until you can afford your own place. Then you can get married sooner. So could your dad and Angie."

"The lead problem is resolved!" Topher said. "When Paul stopped by yesterday to give us a quote, he said he'd cut forty percent off if he could do it that afternoon, as it would save a trip charge.

It was an easy fix, and he had the needed parts with him. I approved, and it's done. All we need to do is get the water tested, which I requested for Monday."

"Okay, then," Emma said. "Let me get Frederick's approval for you to live in the High Priest's residence. Then we can discuss the ceremony."

"Or you and Ash can just talk about it this afternoon. I hear you have an outing planned. But for now, I need to kick you out of the car for my next batch of drivers." Topher looked at his schedule. "It's Nicholas, Kayla, and Grace. I'm covering the rest of the driving sessions this afternoon to give Dad and Angie some time together.

As Emma's three friends walked to the car, she and Montgomery walked away. She had an hour and a half before Ashley arrived to take her and Montgomery to puppy school.

When Emma ate lunch with the priests, she told them about her idea for a test on the Holy Text. Since each priest had an assigned section of Scripture to cover when she gave them a topic to research, she suggested they each submit two questions from their portion. They agreed and promised to do it that afternoon. "No rush," Emma said.

"Monday will be fine." She flashed them a wink and left.

As Ashley drove Emma and Montgomery to puppy school, she prepped Emma on Montgomery's training.

Once there, Montgomery picked up where he left off with his former master. And Emma quickly got up to speed. She now saw just how valuable puppy school would be—for them both.

After the training, Emma stocked up on Montgomery's food, and Ashley paid for it.

"I found an app that will let me transfer money from my account to yours," Emma said. "I just can't use it to make purchases. But the good news is, I have a credit card on the way."

Ashley raised her eyebrows. "I thought they declined you."

"They did, but the next day they emailed me. They said the software didn't know I was the High Priestess and apologized for the error. I'm approved, and my card should arrive on Monday!"

"That's good news."

"Speaking of good news," Emma said, "Topher asked me to officiate your wedding. So we're good to go. I also told him I thought you could stay in the High Priest's residence until you can get your own place. That means you can get married right away."

"Seriously? I'd say let's do it next weekend, but I need to buy a wedding dress and finalize who will be my bridesmaids. And there's a banquet hall to rent and cake and—"

"Assuming you're okay doing a scriptural wedding like we talked about, you won't need any of those things."

Ashley perked up. "Tell me more."

"First, you won't need a wedding dress. You and Topher will both wear wedding robes, kind of like what the priests wear—only nicer. And there will be no bridesmaids or groomsmen. Your parents will stand with you. As far as a fancy wedding cake, the celebrations in the Holy Text don't mention special food. They just served regular food—but lots of it. We can hold the service in the old sanctuary and have the party in the cafeteria, so that will save on renting a hall."

Ashley beamed. "That takes so much pressure off me—and my mom. And I'm sure Dad will appreciate all the money he'll save. They'll be happy to stand with me at the wedding."

Then Ashley's countenance fell. "But Topher's mom died when he was young. I'm not sure what he'll think about only having his dad stand with him."

"What about asking Angie to take part? She'll soon be his stepmom."

"You know about that?"

"Topher told me their good news, but that they're waiting for you to get married first. Was that what you two were talking about at the salon when I came in for my trim? I knew I'd interrupted something important."

"To save money, we were talking about a double wedding. But we didn't want to detract from each other's special day."

Ashley gasped as they arrived at the main entrance to the palace grounds. In the two hours since they'd been gone, a protest march had formed.

"Why don't you let me out here, and I'll try to talk to them," Emma said.

"Is that wise?"

"Not to worry," Emma said. "The Sovereign will protect me. But please alert security, just the same."

19: CLUELESS

About twenty men—yes, they were all men—marched along the road next to the Temple ground's entrance. Since they weren't Temple priests, their protest signs made no sense to Emma: "Protect the Priesthood," "Education Matters," and "We Won't Stand for It."

As Emma approached, trying to appear friendly, they glared at her. When they noticed Montgomery trotting at her side, worry faded from their faces. They stopped chanting. A few even smiled. Emma fell into step with the one she suspected might be their leader.

"What's up?"

"Don't be coy," the man answered. "You know."

Emma shook her head. "I don't. That's why I'm asking."

"Your name, High Priestess, is on the open letter posted on the Temple website about the future of the priesthood. We won't stand for it."

Emma didn't know about any posting, but she suspected it was what she and Jennifer had agreed to on Friday. "We're just trying to be transparent. What's your concern?"

"We have many. For me personally, it's that you're dismissing my seminary training and won't let me be a priest here."

"That's not our intent at all," Emma said. "Anyone can apply to be a priest. There will be an application to complete and a test to take. It's about the Holy Text. For anyone who doesn't pass, we'll offer a one-year accelerated course to get them up to speed."

"We didn't cover the Holy Text in seminary. I don't think anyone did. That's why I'm so angry."

"What about these other guys?"

"I'm not sure why they're here," the man said. "I doubt they know either. But I think someone's paying them to march. Someone with a lot of money."

"Why are you here?"

"I came for clarification about the posting, but I couldn't find anyone to talk to. I guess because it's a Saturday. So I joined the protest."

"How about we go to my office and discuss this?"

The man relaxed, and his expression softened. "I'd like that."

The pair began ascending the long driveway to reach the campus, while the protestors resumed their march. Emma and the man hadn't gone twenty steps when a security guard drove down the hill and offered them a ride.

"Let me send a quick text to my friend," Emma said. "Then we can talk."

The security guard drove up the hill and escorted them to Emma's office. He stationed himself outside.

"I'm curious," Emma said. "Why do you want to be a priest?"

"It seems strange to say, but I think the Sovereign wants me to be one. I went to seminary because I thought it was a good career move. But with all the reforms you're making, I now see that being a priest is not a job but a ministry."

In the spiritual realm, the man had a faint color to his essence. That was good enough for Emma.

"Next week, we should have an application form up on our website. Please fill it out. That's the first step. Then there will be a test to take about the Holy Text. Maybe you can be in the first class. I hope to start soon."

"I'm sure I'll fail the test."

"No worries," Emma said. "That's what the training is for."

The man smiled and then stood. He extended his hand. "My name is Ethan."

"I look forward to receiving your application." Emma smiled and shook his hand.

As he left, Scarlett Steele rushed up, with her cameraman panting behind her. Ethan held up his hand to hide his face. Scarlett motioned for the cameraman to ignore Ethan and follow her into Emma's office. "Your text message surprised me, but thanks for the heads up."

"You'd have heard about the protest anyway, and I wanted to make sure you were the first one on the scene."

"I appreciate that."

"Do you know what's going on?" Emma asked. "The man I just talked to wants to go to our Temple school and become a priest, but he's not sure what the other protesters want."

"I don't think they know either," Scarlett said. "None of them would talk to me. They're pretty much clueless. They focused on marching and chanting, which will make for some good B-roll footage for my coverage."

"The man who just left suspected they were paid protesters."

"That makes sense," Scarlett said. "While I was trying to talk to them, a bus dropped off forty more. They carried the exact same signs—like they were all made at the same time by the same person."

"You said you wanted to do investigative journalism," Emma said. "One idea is to dig into why they're here and who's behind it."

"One idea? You have more?"

Emma nodded. "Though I can't give you my source, some district officials were at Riverside High yesterday looking into records about our microschool and the students who attend. I think someone wants to shut us down."

"Do you know who?" Scarlett asked.

Emma shook her head. "No, but I suspect it comes directly from the Prime Minister herself. She was here on Thursday and threatened me."

Scarlett gasped. "Were there any witnesses?"

Emma shook her head again. "It's her word against mine."

"That certainly explains her impromptu press conference on Friday."

"What?" Emma exclaimed. "I'm almost afraid to ask, but what did she say?"

"She said she met with you on Thursday and has serious concerns about your ability to lead. To restore our revered traditions, she said she'd entertain a bill that only men can serve as High Priests and must be eighteen years old."

This news angered Emma, but it didn't surprise her.

After a pause, Scarlett interviewed Emma for her coverage about the protesters.

When Scarlett finished, Emma had a surprise question of her own. "The priests objected to the room I was living in and insisted I move. Yesterday a room opened. Would you like to see it?"

As they walked to the priests' quarters, Emma gave Scarlett the background. "The space was originally for Barney Clark for those nights he stayed on campus. But one room wasn't enough for him, so he expanded into the room next to his and the room next to it. I'm going to have it turned back into three separate rooms and use the first one for myself. For the last couple of weeks, Gabe—my mentor and one of our spiritual instructors—stayed there. But he's now living with his son."

Emma opened the door to her new room. The cameraman walked in first and spun to record Emma and Scarlett entering. The room was as large, bright, and airy as Emma's former room was small, dark, and dingy.

A large bed occupied one corner of the rectangular space, a nice desk sat in the second, and a sofa, chair, and coffee table in the third. A large bathroom was built into the fourth corner. "I appreciate it the most," Emma said as she pointed to the door. "I'm a bit claustrophobic, and the other shower was so tight that my elbows hit both walls when I washed my hair." She shuddered at the thought.

20: JUST A TEST

After supper, Emma fed Montgomery and walked him. With him now settled for the night, she prayed about the Sunday services, that her part would go well, that the people would benefit from being there, and mostly that the Sovereign would be honored.

An hour later she closed her copy of the Holy Text and laid her journal of notes on top of it. At last she was ready to sleep. Montgomery waited on her bed, his tail wagging as she approached. Ashley was right. She enjoyed snuggling with him.

Slumber awaited and soon it was Sunday.

Though it required careful planning—and involved a bit of jogging—Emma took part in all three Sunday services, even though the traditional service overlapped the two contemporary ones.

The next two days flew by. On Monday, the students and priests took the first draft of the Holy Text test. It was hard, but in a good way. At lunch, Emma's team reviewed and approved Aurora's architectural proposal. And after school, Chloe moved in and became Emma's roommate. By the end of the day Tuesday, Jennifer and Mrs. Butler had finished grading the tests.

On Wednesday, Emma arrived at school early. She wanted to focus on preparing for her weekly update to her disciples. At 8:00 sharp, she stood before them. "I'm excited about the areas you want to work in. If you're still not sure, don't worry. We have time—lots of it—to figure it out. And if you change your mind, you can switch. No problem."

Emma already knew Chloe, Joshua, William, Lane, and Kayla's selections.

Isabella wanted to work in the welcome center when it was finished, Grace saw herself giving tours in the ancient temple, and Lauren wanted to serve at the traditional service.

Natalie saw herself working in the clinic, with the goal of becoming the office manager one day.

Nicholas hoped to be part of the grounds crew. Only Tyler and Dylan remained undecided.

"I also want each one of you to have a priest mentor you, just like Gabe mentors me. Think about who you might like to ask. Or one of them might approach you. I want it to be informal. The most important thing is that you and your mentor are a good fit."

As Emma returned to her seat, Jennifer stood to address the class. "I know the test on the Holy Text really challenged you—it did me. It was hard. We didn't expect many to pass, so don't feel bad about your score. Just know that by the time you graduate, you'll be able to ace it. We've got plenty of time. Think of this as a learning opportunity and a goal to shoot for."

Jennifer passed out the graded tests, with most every student groaning when they saw their score. "Remember that most of you have only been studying the Holy Text for a few weeks. This includes the priests. Of them, only Mark passed. I didn't pass either, which is why Mrs. Butler—and not me—is teaching you about the Holy Text."

Jennifer scanned her students. "I'm pleased to say that everyone did very well on the questions covering what you've already studied. This is a great start, and you should be pleased with your results. I am."

Jennifer paused to let everyone consider what she had said. "There are, however, four people who did exceptionally well. They've been studying the Holy Text much longer. They each scored over 90 percent, which is what we expect for anyone who wants to teach the Holy Text or give a message at one of our services."

"I know it's not me," Lane called out, "but tell us who."

Everyone laughed.

Jennifer smiled. "Drum roll, please."

Lane began drumming his desk with his fingers and everyone joined him.

Jennifer inhaled, her eyes open wide to build anticipation, but she didn't say a thing.

All drumming stopped.

"Mark had an excellent score of 90 percent. Joshua was next at 93. And Emma got a 98. Who do you think was the highest?" Jennifer glanced around the room. When no one guessed, she announced who. "Gabe earned ninety-nine out of one hundred."

Emma didn't even know Gabe took the test, but

it made sense he scored the highest. He'd been studying the Holy Text longer than she'd been alive.

"There's one question everyone got wrong," Jennifer said. "What's interesting is that Emma and Gabe both gave the same answer. Mrs. Butler and I think their answer may be the better response."

Emma thought she knew which question they were talking about and flipped to that page in her test. It was the one that explored Avraham's obedience to the Sovereign's call to become a prophet. In red pen, Mrs. Butler had written, "Though this isn't the response we expected, we'll need to give your answer serious consideration. Well done!"

"Tomorrow we'll resume our studies as usual," Jennifer said, "but for the rest of the morning, I'd like to gather your feedback about the test so we can fine-tune it and make a final version."

21: TOP TEN

That afternoon, Emma met with Jennifer, Mrs. Butler, and Mark to discuss the applications for the first adult priest training class.

"We received hundreds of applications," said Mark, the Chief of Priests. "But since our first class needs to be local, that eliminated many of them. We also ruled out all the teens who applied, since we won't open applications to high schoolers until next year. Of those who are local and adult, I'd like to discuss ten who stood out." Mark passed out a list.

Emma scanned the names. The first five were current Temple employees. She felt each one had the potential to become a priest.

"The last five are interesting," Mark said. "First up is Olivia Fontaine."

"She was a student of mine several years ago," Mrs. Butler said. "I know people can change, but back then she cared only about her appearance and her image."

"Olivia was one of the witnesses who agreed to testify against Barney Clark and changed her mind. He paid her off," Emma said, "but she felt guilty for caving in."

"In her application essay she wrote that her life was a mess," Mark added, "but when Emma accepted her for who she was and offered her grace for what she did, she had hope for the first time in a long time. She wants to be a priest to help others who are hurting and serve here as a counselor in our clinic."

"I have a good feeling about her," Jennifer said.

Mark continued his review. "Our next applicant is most unlikely. She's a waitress Emma interacted with at a local diner. Her name is Zoe. She wrote that Emma didn't judge her for her appearance and treated her with respect. That helped her realize she could become more and didn't need to stay at a job she didn't like. Because of Emma, she now dreams of making a difference. As a priest, she sees herself working behind the scenes in food services."

"She doesn't look like a priest or act like one," Emma said, "and I think she'd be about perfect!"

"Third is someone Emma recommended," Mark said. "His name is Jerry. He's not local but pledged to move here if accepted. He was a guard at the prison and helped Emma free the prisoners. Based on his lengthy essay, she had quite an impact on him. He wants to become a priest to help others grow in their faith."

"I see a lot of potential in him," Emma said.

Mark continued. "Next up is Ethan. He was one of the protesters here on Saturday—and the only one who would talk to Emma. He said he went to seminary for the prestige but now sees becoming a priest as a mission and not a career. His chat with Emma confirmed that."

"He said he learned nothing about the Holy Text in seminary," Emma added. "We can help with that."

"Last is the most surprising applicant," Mark said. "It's Michael Johnson—the principal at Riverside High."

Emma gasped.

"On his application he said he's disillusioned

with his job. He said that politics is supplanting what's best for the students. He laments giving in to pressure and not protecting Emma at school or her friends after she left. If he's accepted into the program, he will resign immediately."

"When I tried to return to Riverside after becoming the High Priestess," Emma said, "he apologized for not doing more to stop the harassment. He said, 'my hands are tied.' So that might be what he's talking about."

"I understand where he's coming from," Mrs. Butler said. "He's an honorable man of integrity and perfect for the priesthood."

"What's noteworthy," Mark said, "is that all ten applicants mentioned Emma in their essay for the positive impact she's had on them. She was instrumental in them wanting to become priests. I recommend we accept all ten."

"Should they take the test first?" Mrs. Butler asked.

"I'm afraid that will scare them away," Emma said. "Let's only give the test to people who think they don't need to learn about the Holy Text."

Everyone agreed.

With the first group of students selected, they were ready to restart the Temple school to train priests. Emma could cross another item off her to-do list.

She thought about all she had done—with the Sovereign's help. The priests now focused on studying the Holy Text, they served in their areas of interest and expertise, and they went about their day with a greater sense of purpose. They were making a difference.

Together they were moving forward in perfecting the priesthood. This would grow the Sovereign's kingdom and honor their Lord. And it was just the beginning.

If you enjoyed *Perfecting the Priesthood*, please leave a review online. Your review will help others learn about this book and encourage them to read it too.

Thank you.

Chapter 1: Arrested

Emma Barlow pulled out her phone to silence it when a text came in. It was from Michael Johnson, the principal at Riverside High, the school she had attended before becoming the High Priestess. *He's never texted me. Something's up.*

Emma read the text. "May the Sovereign bless you today at school."

Less than a week ago, he had warned her that the government might try to shut down their microschool. He also said he didn't dare text her, which would create a record that could be used against him. Since he texted her today, it must be important. Really important. Emma concluded that today was the day when it all might come down.

She sent a quick text alerting Hernandez, the chief of security. As an afterthought, she also texted Scarlett Steele, the reporter assigned to cover her and everything that happened on the Temple grounds. Once finished, Emma shoved her phone into the back pocket of her jeans.

Sitting in the classroom of her microschool, Emma waited for her teacher to arrive. To her left sat her bestie, Chloe. They were roommates during the week. To her right sat her boyfriend, Joshua. Their ten friends—her disciples—sat scattered behind them. Her puppy, Montgomery, hadn't gone to doggie daycare, so he snuggled in his favorite spot in the back corner.

Jennifer arrived to signal the beginning of school, yet most of the students had already begun their assignments. As for Emma, her algebra book lay open in front of her, but she couldn't focus. Instead of worrying about what might happen, she prayed instead, asking for the Sovereign's divine protection for her, her friends, and their microschool. Peace flooded her being.

With her focus restored, she began working through her algebra problems. But a commotion soon interrupted her. Alarmed, Emma turned around. There stood an uptight-looking woman wearing an ill-fitting business suit. Two police officers flanked her.

"May I help you?" Jennifer asked. Their teacher moved toward the unwelcome guests.

"We're here to observe your so-called school," the woman said. "I'm authorized by district headquarters and acting on behalf of the capital."

"You need to schedule your observations with me in advance." Jennifer moved closer to them. "Your presence is interrupting my students. I insist you leave immediately."

"Though we often extend the courtesy, we're not required to provide advance notice." The woman planted her fist on her hip and scowled. "The urgency of the situation required immediate action. We must protect the children."

Hernandez burst into the room, but one of the police officers held up his left hand while placing his right hand on his holstered sidearm. Hernandez halted his approach while his gaze darted around the room.

Emma stood and moved toward her teacher to confront the threat. "In the name of the Sovereign, I command you to leave."

The woman laughed. "I care nothing about the Sovereign or your antiquated beliefs. Your idle threats mean nothing to me."

Emma edged up to Jennifer.

The other police officer stepped toward Emma while avoiding eye contact. "With all due respect, High Priestess," he said with a slight bow, "I will detain you if needed." He reached for Emma's shoulder to push her away from Jennifer.

A yipping Montgomery raced to the officer and nipped at his ankle. The guard swung his leg to kick the tiny puppy, but Montgomery was too fast.

"Leave my dog alone!" Emma lunged toward the officer, but Joshua's muscular arms pulled her back. He spun Emma away from the officer and stepped toward the uniformed man.

The officer glared at Joshua. "Do you want me to arrest you?"

"It wouldn't be the first time I was arrested for protecting Emma." Joshua stomped closer to the officer and glared back.

"I've seen enough of this circus," the stern woman stated. "There is no education occurring here. This is not a school. It's nothing more than a ruse to circumvent these children from receiving their legally mandated education." The woman jabbed her finger at Jennifer. "You're no teacher. You're nothing but a fraud."

Jennifer held her ground. "I suggest you familiarize yourself with how a microschool functions. Not only are these students excelling at their work, they're also ahead of where they should be at this point in the school year."

The woman shook her head. "You're only allowed to have ten students. I count thirteen. That puts you in violation."

"She's not our only teacher," Emma interjected. "We also have Elizabeth Butler here on staff."

The woman shook her head. "Not according to my records. And that's all that matters." She nodded to the police officer standing nearest her.

"Jennifer Russell," the man said, "I'm placing you under arrest."

Continue this story in *Pursuing the Politicians*, book 8 of The Next High Priest Series.

ABOUT PETER DEHAAN

Peter DeHaan is an adult who dreams of being a teenager. When he's not contemplating grown-up thoughts, his mind retreats to the domain of invented worlds with his loyal and most real, yet still imaginary, friends. What grand adventures they have: righting wrongs, solving problems, and making their world a better place to live.

His first published adventures come to life in "The Next High Priest Series"—a faith-friendly speculative fiction adventure in a world just like ours . . . only different.

Next up is *The Curious Gift*, a YA contemporary novella with a hint of the supernatural.

Then comes "The Ice Creamed Series," a present-day quest for friendship and love, all the while trying to survive high school unscathed and ping-ponging between responsible impulses and irresponsible slipups.

Want more? Get a free short-story prequel about Emma along with news of upcoming books when you sign up to receive updates at PeterDeHaan.com/fiction.

FICTION BOOKS BY PETER DEHAAN

The Next High Priest Series

Seeking the Sovereign

Confronting the Chaos

Dueling the Devil

Reforming the Religion

Freeing the Prisoners

Fighting the Fanatics

Perfecting the Priesthood

Pursuing the Politicians

Restoring the Repentant

Learn more at PeterDeHaan.com/fiction.